Den of Sins

A Dark Mafia Romance

Chicago Sin
Book 1

Alta Hensley

Renee Rose

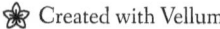 Created with Vellum

Want FREE Renee Rose books?

also get bonus epilogues, special pricing, exclusive previews and news of new releases.

Chapter One

A rmando

Is a sinner ever free?

Regardless of the answer, I'm as close as you can get. I'm no longer trapped in a cage.

The prison gates open, and I walk out with nothing but a paper bag that contains the few belongings I came in with.

My cousin, Marco, waits for me, standing in front of his SUV with an overly expressive smile on his face. I know him well enough to see right through it. Sure, he's happy to see me, but he's obviously uncomfortable.

Can't say I blame him.

Marco visited me here on occasion. He would drive up from Chicago, our hometown an hour away, to spend an hour updating me on what was going on with the Outfit. He, and sometimes his brother Leo, are the only ones who visited out of the *La Famiglia*.

Again, something I understood.

Prison could be contagious. No one wants to catch it.

It's a plague that once transmitted is hard to treat.

Even my mother didn't visit—not being able to handle seeing her son treated like an animal. Her words, not mine.

As I hesitate outside of the prison gates, Marco eventually steps forward, breaking the silence. "It's good to see you," he says, finally giving up his painted smile.

"Yeah." I'm not sure I'm up for small talk yet.

Marco seems to understand and moves on quickly, motioning to the car. "Come on, let's get you out of here."

We both climb into the vehicle, and Marco starts the drive back to the city.

I stare out the window, seeing nothing. Apparently hearing nothing until I realize Marco has been talking the whole time.

"...when you hit Rocco's for a haircut and shave Friday. It's the same old crew, of course, but I'll bet they give you priority in the barber's chair.... The florist shop is still next door, but Mary Alice sold the place to her apprentice, Hannah. Remember her? She was just a kid when you left, but she's hot as fuck now...."

I tune him out. The places he's talking about–our old familiar haunts–seem so far away and removed right now. I guess I'll have to go there to feel anything.

"Some shit's changed since you've been away," Marco observes.

I don't answer, waiting for him to go on.

"The Outfit's getting more and more powerful, but it's losing its soul. A lot of the Made men are getting complacent. There's no more progress, you know? No old soul wisdom, as the don calls it."

I absorb his words without comment. Marco is a smart guy. There's no one whose opinion I respect more, especially when it comes to Family business. He came into the

Outfit about the same time I did, but he has good insight into it. He is far wiser than his age or experience.

He definitely possesses the old soul wisdom. Marco seems to be able to look at the organization objectively and notice what's really going on.

I try to focus on his words, on work, and on what will be my reality again now that I'm back in the fold of the family, but I fight an overwhelming tightness in my chest.

The sides of the SUV feel suffocating, reminding me of the prison cell.

I take a deep breath and crack the window. It's been a long time since I've been around anyone who hasn't been jaded by the system. People in prison speak differently than people who are free.

Getting used to Marco—getting used to anyone—is going to be a challenge.

Fifty-four months. That's how long I served in the state pen. My colorless existence between four concrete walls.

Longer than some members of the Outfit served. Shorter than others. I kept my mouth shut and did the time like I was supposed to. I also earned a business degree.

"Out on good behavior," Marco huffs, as if he's reading my mind. "Who would have thought?"

I don't answer but think how ironic that is since I literally shanked a man in prison. Thankfully, I'm a Made Man, and the don kept me protected and out of trouble. Amazing how the mafia has the ability to make things simply disappear on the inside. The power inside the system may even be stronger than outside the concrete walls.

Noticing the white knuckles of Marco's hands as he grips the steering wheel, I see I'm making him uncomfortable. I know why. I got pinched, and he didn't. I served time while he remained free. I've felt the same way before. A

3

survivor's guilt of sorts when one of your own goes down for a family crime. It's hard to face, and there is always a part of you that wonders when you'll be next. It's cliche to say that prison changes a man, but it's fucking true.

Now, riding passenger in my cousin Marco's car back in Chicago, I don't experience the big joy of freedom. I note the sky. Tall buildings. The traffic. The noise and energy of the city that ate me up and shit me out. It elicits nothing. The familiar streets, familiar places evoke nothing of my old self. Of the young man I was before I did time. I've been numb the whole ride, having some kind of out-of-body experience with being on the outside. I've thought of this day since the day I went in, but now that it's here, now that I'm out... I feel nothing at all. I'm dead to the experience.

"Hey, let's stop for dinner. My treat, obviously." He maneuvers his SUV to parallel park in front of Lorenzo's Italian restaurant, one of the Outfit's favorite haunts.

"Sure, yeah." I don't want to. The silent car ride was excruciating enough. I appreciate Marco's loyalty to me, but I'd rather not have to spend another hour with him. I don't want to see anyone I used to know.

But I always did love eating at Lorenzo's. The food is served in large portions, and everyone is treated like a guest of the house, especially if you're part of the Outfit. The waiters and staff used to know me by name, greeting me with enthusiastic handshakes and hugs. It'll be interesting to see if anything has changed.

An explosion of voices assaults me as I step inside.

I have no weapon. I have no way to fight.

Chapter Two

*A*rmando

My whole body goes rigid, my instinct to fight for my life activated before I can turn it off.

"Bentornato!" Welcome back. Cheers of celebration follow.

Fuck.

Bentornato, Mando, the giant banner spanning the private room reads.

Everyone shouts and claps around me as I struggle to exhale the breath lodged under my ribs. They're focused on me with welcoming faces, but I can't make my face crack even the semblance of a smile for the assholes.

"Cristo, you coulda warned me," I mutter to Marco. We're six months apart, me and him. Raised together. Fought together. We became Made Men together. We're tighter than brothers.

And for a split moment... I thought we were going to die together.

He cuts a look at me, taking in my balled fists. The

5

muscle ticking at my jaw. "Surprise," he says sardonically. "Sorry. I'll get you a drink."

My ma throws herself at me, her thin arms strangling my neck. I have to force my fingers open to hold her. I feel too many ribs on her back. Adrenaline's still pumping from the unwelcome fucking surprise.

Seriously. Who gives a new prison-release a *surprise* party? I coulda killed one of them if they were within swinging distance. Thank God Marco didn't give me a gun when he picked me up.

I scan the room filled with familiar faces.

Don Pachino sits in the back, chewing on a cigar and sipping whiskey, his capos and son-in-law beside him. I lift my chin to him across the room to show respect, and he raises his glass.

It's a soldier's welcome: the hero's return.

Except only the people in this room will treat me like a hero. To the rest of the world, I'm forever marked by my felony conviction.

A criminal.

"You're too thin, Mando," my mother chides when I finally get her to loosen her hold on me.

"So are you, Ma." I kiss her cheek. She's much more bony than when I left. Her hair's going grey, too. It kills me to see how much my stint in prison aged her.

I stare down at the cross around her neck and wonder what she must think of me. It's not often that the son of a devout Catholic ends up in prison. I know I've disappointed her in a way that can never be made right again.

The cross around her neck only serves as a further reminder of how far I have fallen from the altar boy with dreams of one day becoming a priest like my childhood hero, Father Fantoni. The faith he had always preached to me about seemed to have no power in saving me from my own demons and family ties.

My mother stares at me with a mix of love and uncertainty. I can see the fear in her eyes that I could end up back where I just came from, but still she welcomes me with open arms. She loves me despite what I do and who I surround myself with, and for that I am grateful. She's a mother in the mafia, and that comes with a certain amount of baggage but also understanding. But no mother wants to see her son go to prison. I'm supposed to keep what I do secret from her church and the ladies she does lunch with. I'm nót supposed to mess up.

I do want to tell her that I'm sorry for letting her down and that I will try to do better, but it's hard to find the words.

I don't know why stepping into the old place feels like a punch in the gut. This party is for me. I should be celebrating. But I don't remember what joy feels like.

I don't even remember what it means to feel.

Father Fantoni approaches, and though I'm surprised to see him at the party, I know he's no stranger to the Outfit. He's seen us all grow from children and is just as much family as anyone else in this room.

"I hope to see you at Sunday Service now," he says as he places a welcoming hand on my shoulder. "Welcome home."

There is no judgment in his eyes. No condemnation.

"Yes, Father. As soon as I get... settled."

Seemingly satisfied with my answer, he nods and continues making his rounds in the room.

"Good to see you, Mando." A sweet feminine voice murmurs at my shoulder.

I turn to take in the practiced beauty of my ex. Her perfect makeup, straightened hair. Big green doe-eyes.

Fucking Grace.

Oddly, I feel nothing. Not rage. Not pain. Not betrayal.

I flatline on any response, so I turn and hit her with full eye contact. "You didn't have to come."

"Course I did." Her fingers tangle and fight each other in front of her waist. She's in high heels and a blue polka-dot wrap-around that shows off her perfect tits, with a diamond heart necklace dangling above them. A necklace I sure as hell didn't give her. Ten feet behind her stands Emilio, her new conquest. Or maybe he conquered her—what do I know?

All I know is she didn't even bother showing up in person to return my engagement ring.

"No. You really didn't." I say it pointed-like, and color leeches from her face.

"If you want me to leave, I will," she whispers, lips trembling.

There was a time seeing those green eyes shining with tears would make me move mountains to comfort her. Now, I feel nothing at her distress. I just shrug. "I don't give a shit either way, doll."

I push past her and make my way to the don. His salt and pepper hair has also grown more salty, but he still looks every inch the reigning king. The godfather of the Outfit, if you will.

He's the only one I have to respect here. The one I owe my loyalty to. The rest of these *stronzos* can fuck themselves.

Aside from my cousins, no one in this room bothered to visit me during my stay in the pen. Why are they acting like they care now?

"Mando. Sit." Don Pachino pats the barstool beside him. I'm not sure if I should be offended that he didn't stand up to embrace me. I drop into the seat and offer my hand. He tucks the cigar between his teeth and squeezes my palm too hard, like he used to when I was a teen. Showing me who's boss.

Alex, his son-in-law, moves away to give us privacy.

"Care for one?" He slides the cigar box in my direction. I should take it. I should light up and smoke with the don. Show I'm still his trusted lieutenant. Prove my loyalties haven't changed.

But the smell turns my stomach. "No thanks." I rub my nose like that will clear the stench. "Too early."

Marco presses a high-ball glass of Maker's Mark into my hand and disappears again, slick-like, before I remember to thank him. I throw it back, relishing the burn as it slides down my throat.

"So, you're out."

"*Si signore.* Glad to be back."

It's not true. I'm not glad to be anything. *Glad* isn't an emotion I've known for a very long time. But it's what I'm supposed to say.

Don Pachino pulls a thick envelope from the inner pocket of his five-thousand-dollar suit and hands it to me. "This is to get you on your feet again."

I tuck it in the pocket of the jacket Marco brought me when he picked me up. The one that feels so foreign on me, even though it was my favorite.

"Thank you, Don Pachino."

He takes a puff of the cigar. "I got you a no-work construction job. Pays six grand a month. You're taken care of, Mando."

I bow my head, the gratitude I should show not surfacing. I have to fake it. "Thank you. I'm so grateful."

He claps me on the shoulder. "I told you I'd take care of you, didn't I? You're family, Mando."

"I appreciate that. So much." Jesus, I hope my tone doesn't sound as flat to his ears as it does to mine.

I don't mean to look, but somehow, I find myself staring across the room at Grace, rubbing her tits over Emilio's chest.

"You were gone," Don Pachino says with finality. He's making it clear where he stands on the issue in case I'm gonna make waves.

I don't answer because what the fuck am I going to say? *Yeah, it's cool he stole my fucking fiancé while I was doing time like a good soldier*. Sorry if I don't go kiss his cheeks and let him fuck me in the ass some more while he's at it.

Don Pachino doesn't take kindly to my silence. His casual air evaporates, and he looks me square in the eye. "There will be no retribution for it. *Capisce?*"

I only hesitate a moment before I nod. One thing I always respected about Don Pachino—he's damn clear about his expectations. "Understood."

"Do not test me on this."

"I won't."

"We're Family. All of us." He gestures around the room with his cigar. I wait for him to finish his point, but all he mutters is, "And you were gone."

Yeah.

Got the memo.

I was gone. My girl was fair game.

Now I know how things get played.

I definitely feel disrespected by both of them, but the truth is, no hearts were broken.

I may have thought I loved Grace when I left, but that shriveled and died long before I got the news about her new engagement. It died that first year in prison when she stopped writing and never came to see me.

"I want you to stay clean while you're on parole. You ride that no-work job and build your life again. Don't carry a piece or drive a car or violate the other terms of parole. I don't want you getting sent back for something stupid."

"I'm not going back," I agree.

No fucking way.

Not because I'm so goddamn happy to be out. I still can't dredge up a single lick of emotion.

But I'm damn sure I won't go back.

I'd rather take a bullet to the head.

Chapter Three

H*annah*
Hannah Munn, Florist to the mob.
That's me.

Say what you will about the mafia, but there are a few perks to having your business in their building. One is the regular customers—which I desperately need.

My shop, *Garden of Eden,* is a place that allows the sins of the mafia to grow.

And if I don't sell five more bouquets by the time I close tonight, I won't be able to make my payment to the don.

And the simmering anxiety that brings would be the downside to being owned by the mafia.

"I need two bouquets. A big one for my wife, and—"

"And a smaller one for the girlfriend," I finish for Lorenzo, the cheating bastard. It's the same every week. "Some beautiful lavender roses came in yesterday. I made you a stunning bouquet for the wife." I walk to the cooler and pull out the arrangement—a dozen fat lavender roses with pink and purple freesia and greens.

Because I believe flowers mean something, I put a lot of

effort into Lorenzo's wife's bouquets. Like, if I get the arrangement right, if I really wow her, it will make up for her husband's infidelity. Although maybe she's off with her own side piece—what do I know? She could have some hot pool boy or sexy yoga teacher licking her from toes to clit right now. I shouldn't care about someone I know nothing about, and yet I do. I take on other's emotions to a crippling degree sometimes. Always a people pleaser.

"And this one is for the girl *du jour.*" I hand him a bouquet of brightly colored gerbera daisies.

Lorenzo cocks a half-smile like he's not sure what *du jour* means. Or maybe he's wondering if I'm being disrespectful. Hope not. I flash a bright smile to assure him I'm trying for cute.

I head back to the cash register and ring him up. Lorenzo's been coming here since before Mary Alice hired me as an apprentice ten years ago when I was just a teenager.

Every Friday, he and a half dozen of the Pachino men go see Rocco, the barber next door, for a straight razor shave, then hit *Garden of Eden* to get blooms for their ladies. Another crew comes through on Thursdays. And the older, retired generation usually stops in on Saturdays. One thing about these mafia men I've noticed is they like their structure and routine.

"Keep the change, doll." All these years, and he never bothered to learn my name. Or if he has, he never uses it. He pushes the six dollars and coins back across the counter. "It's your hush money." He winks. Same joke, every time. Every. Single. Time.

"Thank you, Lorenzo." I drop the money back in the till. Lord knows I'll need it to cover the checks I've already written that may already be bouncing me straight to bankruptcy. Or worse, getting my kneecaps busted by one of the very same customers I'm giving thanks for.

"You heard from Mary Alice?"

I smile, indulgently. I suspect Mary Alice was Lorenzo's girl *du jour* a few times over the years, but my former boss would never tell. Florists are excellent secret-keepers.

"Yeah." I spin one of the roses in his bouquet to set it at a better angle. "She texts photos of her grandbaby pretty much every day. She's in seventh heaven out there." Mary Alice moved to Green Bay when her daughter had a baby last year, forcing me to choose between continuing my studies to become a nurse like my mom or buying the business from her.

My parents definitely think I made the wrong choice. They don't say that outright—they're more the type to let me make my own mistakes, but I sense their worry every time the topic comes up.

I'm starting to wonder if I made a mistake too.

"Well, you tell her I said hello." He tucks the two bouquets under his arm and pushes his wallet back into his pocket.

"I'll do that. Have a great weekend."

He starts to leave then turns back. "Everything okay around here? Anybody bothering you?"

I shoot a glance at Josie, my BFF-slash-slacker employee who's putting a chrysanthemum arrangement in the cooler. She smirks because we just had this conversation. These guys like to play hero.

"Everything's fine. But thanks for asking." My smile is genuine because as much as I like to roll my eyes and snark about my customers, I'm secretly fond of them. Probably because when I was fifteen, their five-dollar tips made me feel rich. And the romantic florist in me still appreciates their chivalry.

I like the safety of being on their watch. Knowing if something did go wrong—if I got held up or I had a stalker situation—I'd know exactly who to see to exact justice.

Lorenzo tips an invisible hat and leaves, and Josie snorts. "You're right."

I laugh. "Did I not tell you? At least one of them will offer to slay dragons for me every week. It's kind of endearing."

"Of course." Josie nearly knocks an arrangement over as she pushes vases around on the cooler shelf. "The idea of roughing up some asshole for the pretty, defenseless florist gets them hard."

"Mmm hmm. Cute, right?"

"Yeah, I guess you can't complain about having your own private security team. And at least he wasn't creepy about it. One dumbass yesterday bought flowers and then pulled out a rose and gave it to me. I was like, dude, if you're going to ask for my number at least give me the whole bouquet."

I snort. "Yeah, they're players." When I was in high school, I used to get all fluttery and nervous when the younger guys came in, thinking one might ask me out. I had this whole mafia-guy crush. They exuded confidence and power. They flashed their money, and they had swagger. I wasn't naive enough to believe all the bluster, but it turned me on just the same. My secret fantasy.

But while they flirted up a storm with Mary Alice, they were only polite with me. I don't know, maybe they don't date Black women. Or maybe I was just a kid in their eyes and forever would be.

"Well, maybe not all of them, but at least half are players," I amend.

Josie comes over and leans her elbows on the counter. Her gold hoop earrings swing. They're giant—big enough to balance her poofy blonde curls.

Anxiety coils in the pit of my stomach as we get physically close to each other. It happens every time. Probably because I need to talk to her about her crappy work ethic but keep putting it off. I ignore the feeling, like always.

"Tell me you haven't thought about taking one of them up on it. Not as a permanent thing but just to let him treat you to a nice dinner once in a while," she says.

"Nah."

"Uh huh." Her tone implies disbelief.

"Okay, there was one, but he had a girlfriend. He never asked me out, but he charmed the socks off me every time he came in. And so good looking. He lectured me once when I was closing up about walking home alone at night and how it wasn't safe. He insisted he escort me the couple of blocks. I found his protectiveness so freaking hot."

"Which one?" Josie asks.

"I don't know. I can't remember his name," I lie. I totally remember. *Armando.* Sexy smooth-talking Armando with that panty-melting smile.

But I was almost grateful he was engaged. Because as much as I crushed on him, I never, ever, want to date a mafia man. They cheat on their wives. They're misogynists —they think women belong barefoot, home in the kitchen. They are dangerous. Extremely so. They commit crimes, they hurt people, even kill people. Yes, they are men, but there's a thick undertone of villain in every single one of them.

And Armando—he felt the most unsafe. Not like he'd hurt me physically.

But emotionally. I'd fall way too hard for a guy like him. It was good he disappeared.

"He doesn't come in anymore. I haven't seen him in a long time—like, years," I tell Josie.

"Maybe he got whacked. You never know with these guys, right?"

I'm way too empathetic because that thought makes my stomach tighten up into a knot. I hardly knew the guy apart from selling him flowers for his fiancé every week. "Hope not. He seemed like he was going places."

"Yep. Illegal places that landed him in Lake Michigan with cement shoes," Josie jokes.

I refuse to entertain that idea. "Maybe he moved away. He and his girlfriend were engaged." I know because he filled her apartment with every color of rose after she said yes. Mary Alice had to call for an extra shipment because he ordered so many.

"I'll bet he's dead. Or witness protection." She shrugs and pushes an unfinished bouquet off to the side. "I'm going to take off, okay?"

My anxiety flutters again. It's forty minutes until her shift ends. She hasn't even finished what she was working on, and her work area is a mess. I definitely need the help in case a bunch of the guys next door stop in to buy bouquets before they go home.

Please, God, let there be a closing time rush.

I should tell her that, but instead, I bite back my sigh. I love her too much to create strife between us. I know— hiring a friend was a mistake. One I'm going to keep paying for if I don't figure out pretty quickly how to be a boss bitch. But Josie got laid off from her dream job as an interior decorator apprentice, so I invited her to work here with me, thinking how fun it would be to run a business with my best friend at my side.

Except it's not always fun. And lately, it's more stressful when she's around than when she's not. It doesn't take a psychotherapist to figure out that's why I get anxious when she's here. My subconscious wants me to clarify things with her, but my heart can't stand the thought of alienating my best friend.

But that's kind of the least of my worries about running this business at this point. And I may not even have a business past next month if things don't turn around.

"Okay thanks."

Ugh. Why am I thanking her? I'm *paying* her. And she's leaving early.

Without asking.

And I now have *her* mess to clean up.

Still, if I had it to do over, I'd probably hire her again because the thought of hiring a stranger makes me way too nervous.

I am so not cut out to be Boss Bitch.

Instead of saying anything more, I look to the door and try to will someone to walk in and order all the flowers I have to offer.

Chapter Four

Armando

"It's not a big apartment," Marco says as he puts the keys into the door and opens it. "But it's down the hall from me, and the building is centrally located."

I take a look around the small apartment. It's simple and cozy, but there are no decorations or any other personal touches. The bedroom is furnished with just a bed, dresser, and a small nightstand. There's a black, leather couch in the living room and a kitchen table in the corner of the room. The only window is in the living room, but there's a balcony outside with a great view of the Chicago skyline.

"You can decorate it however you want, put up whatever pictures you want," Marco says, gesturing to the blank walls. "The landlord is cool here. Also, my lady friend says that she knows a few people who can do interior design for you if you want. I can hook you up with them if you're interested."

I look around the apartment, feeling a bit overwhelmed.

I've been in jail with a cellmate for long enough that the idea of actually being alone for a night is bizarre.

"I know it's not much, but it's a start," Marco says, apparently trying to be encouraging. "Soon you'll be back on your feet, and you can do whatever the fuck you want."

I nod and take a deep breath. "Thanks, Marco." I should show more enthusiasm, but I can't muster it.

Luckily, Leo enters the apartment, his dominance filling the room. During my time in prison, my cousin has grown. He's no longer the scrawny, young, arrogant kid trying to prove himself to the Outfit. He's nearly tripled in size and reminds me of a brick wall. Nothing but brawn strides into the room. I don't think Marco and I combined could take this man down if we tried.

His eyes dart to the balcony. "What the fuck? A balcony? A ladder escape? Are you just inviting someone to come up here and jump him?"

"He's laying low right now," Marco retorts. "It's not like there's a hit on him or anything. Let the man enjoy a view and some fresh air after having gone so long without it."

Leo grunts in hesitant approval, his eyes still scanning the apartment for any threats. He finally turns to me. "Welcome back, cuz. I've missed you." He claps me on the shoulder, his grip strong and comforting. He then narrows his eyes at his brother. "Balconies only bring pigeons. Pigeons bring shit."

"I put beer in the fridge," Marco says as he walks toward the kitchen with an eye roll. "Anyone?"

"Yeah." I need one. I feel completely out of place in what is supposed to be my home.

Leo takes a beer from Marco and tips it toward me. "Cheers, cuz. To a new start."

I take the beer, wanting to savor the taste of freedom, but it tastes as flat as my emotions. Is this freedom?

It's all so strange. I'm out of prison, but I'm not really free. I'm living a life dependent on the generosity and connections of others.

Leo sits on the couch and stretches his legs. "So, Mando," he begins. "You cool with Grace and Emilio? Truly cool?"

"Fuck no." I can actually be honest with my cousins.

Marco grunts his agreement.

"The don says to be cool, so I'm cool. But truth between us, the situation is fucked." I cross over to an armchair next to the couch and sit with my beer as I take a long swig.

"I never liked Grace," Marco offers, leaning up against the kitchen counter. "I wasn't surprised when she went searching for her next meal ticket."

"I don't give a fuck about Grace." Or at least not anymore. "It's fucked that what was mine wasn't protected while I was inside. Emilio stepped in when he should have been watching out. He broke the fucking code, man."

"Yeah, it's bullshit," Leo agrees. "He broke the code for sure. No way to defend that."

"I didn't see it coming," Marco says. "I would have squashed that shit fast if I had."

"Same." Leo's jaw tightens. "Emilio kept that under lock and key. By the time word got out, the don was aware and seemed to give his approval. So..."

"If the don says no retribution..." Marco begins.

"There won't be retribution," I finish.

But that doesn't mean I have to like it. That doesn't mean I have to forget. I take another swig of beer and shake my head.

"Besides. Grace always took me as a lazy fuck. I can't

see her giving good head." Marco smirks, clearly trying to lighten the mood.

Personally I don't agree with knocking a guy's ex because you're basically insulting his taste in the first place, but whatever.

"Yeah, you definitely need to find yourself someone who can meet your sexual appetite. Because after your drought... you gotta be one ravenous motherfucker," Leo adds.

I remember when I used to see men come out of prison and think the same thing. Like the worst thing in the world for these ex-convicts was how long they'd have to go without sex. I'm sure I'd think the same thing as Marco and Leo. Sex is the first priority because how could it not be?

But, shit... I'm not even sure how to start. My entire body feels fucking numb. Including my dick.

"The don gave me some bullshit construction job. It's just for appearances," I tell them. "I show up and collect a check."

"Yeah, I heard that," Marco says.

"Not a bad gig." Leo finishes his beer in one last swig and then motions for Marco to pass him another one.

"It feels as if I've been put to pasture," I admit. "I was in my prime before all this shit. Now, I'm practically retired."

"Temporarily, right?" Marco asks. "Until parole is over?"

I shrug. "My entire life feels temporary. A big fucking pause button was hit when I got pinched. Now what?"

"You need money?" Leo asks.

"Nah." I shake my head. "The don took care of that. And this job puts me in a good spot. But thanks."

The last thing I'd do is take money from my cousins. I feel like a burden as it is.

"You did your time. You didn't snitch. And now you're

back. You've earned some retirement life. Enjoy it while you can. I'm sure that once parole is over, the don will have you working full time, earning again."

"We'll get your life back in order," Marco adds. "It will take some time, but you'll rise from the fucking ashes. I promise."

Chapter Five

Armando

"Armando." Rocco pats the barber chair.

"Right here, sir." I disengage from the gathering of Made men who fill the old-time barber shop with cigar smoke while they talk over each other in loud voices.

The walls are a drab off-white and crammed floor to ceiling with framed photographs from the days when the shop was a speakeasy. Wood paneling, a bay window, old fold out chairs and a magazine rack brings me back to a time I cherished. Each man is dressed in a tailored suit and tie, his hair slicked back, mustache and beard perfectly trimmed and groomed.

Rocco's barbershop is an oasis of the familiar in a world that has become otherwise unfamiliar.

My body's stiff and jerky as I drop into the seat. Every step I take in my old shoes is like a goddamn out-of-body experience.

Coming to this place is an out-of-body experience.

Everything's exactly the same, yet it feels so fucking different. I used to love Friday afternoons in this little shop.

The pleasure of Rocco's warm towels wrapped around my face. Feeling like a king while the old man attended to me with the guys all hanging around shooting the shit. I loved hanging with the big boys. So proud I'd made lieutenant and got to play with the heavy hitters. I was on the top of the world then. Top of my game.

I had the girl. The money. And a glorified position in the Outfit.

I felt alive. Powerful. There was so much possibility dancing before me.

Only thing different now is the girl. But I got over Grace the day she called and told me she was moving in with Emilio. So why the fuck can't I find any pleasure?

Arturo, Don Pachino's right hand man, gives me a scrutinizing look through a billow of smoke. "You don't look comfortable, Mando. Hard to trust someone with a blade close to your throat after sleeping behind bars?"

Flashbacks of when someone actually was foolish enough to try to attack me in prison come flooding in. I had pissed off the wrong person, but he didn't know how lethal I could be. He made the mistake of underestimating me, and he paid for it.

"Don Pachino's been in the business for a long time, Mando. He knows how to pick his men. You have a reputation for being loyal and careful, which is why he trusts you." He pauses and then continues with, "But more than that, he knows you won't hesitate to do whatever it takes to make sure the job gets done. You just need to keep your head in the game. Don't fuck it up again because you allow that darkness in. You know what I mean. Fight it off, son."

I nod and force a smile. "I'm good Arturo. Nothing to worry about."

I take a moment to survey the room. It's still filled with

the same faces. Familiar ones. Ones who have seen me through thick and thin.

But something is off. I feel it in the air. Tension. Skepticism. A lack of trust that never seemed to be there before.

I understand why. I was in prison for a long time, and while I had the support of the Outfit on the inside, there was still some distance kept. Regardless of what they said, I know they viewed me as a liability. There was always a chance I'd rat to save my ass. They also knew I couldn't help them if I was behind bars, so they acted as though I didn't exist.

Now I'm back, and I feel the sizzle of awkwardness in my veins. They don't know me anymore, and I don't know them. We are strangers to one another.

"You know," Arturo begins, "It's not too late to try and make things right again."

I furrow my brow in confusion. Make what right? What the hell was he talking about? Make Grace come back? Make the don forget I ever went to prison? Make my incarceration disappear?

Arturo continues, "The don loves you. We all do. You were born for this, Mando. You're the best of the best. And you should never forget that. You're still young, you can make it back to the top. Everyone knows it."

I close my eyes, feeling the warmth from the hot towels against my face. I feel the sharpness of the blades against my throat, a reminder that I'm still here. Alive and breathing. As much as it pains me to admit it, I know Arturo is right. I clawed my way back from the bottom and am still standing. As long as I'm alive, I can make it to the top. But at the same time, I've been grounded by the don himself. Ordered to keep my nose clean.

The pull of good and evil is strong. The devil on one shoulder and the angel on the other is now my reality.

It takes all my effort to twist a smile onto my face. It's probably more of a grimace.

Arturo's statement brings an awkward pause in conversation. It's mostly the oldtimers today with only me, Marco and Leo representing the younger generation. I suspect someone told Emilio to stay away out of respect for me today. Probably Marco. He looks after me like a second brother. I'd do the same for him if the tables were turned.

"I'll bet that shave is gonna feel good, right kid?" one of them says.

"You wet your dick yet?" Angel, another oldtimer, asks. "*Madonna,* when I got out, I picked up a girl at the strip club and banged her all night long. *For three nights!*" His boom of laughter is joined by several of the other guys'.

I go tense although I don't know why I'm defensive. Because the thought of fucking doesn't get the slightest rise out of me? Because *life* gets zero rise out of me?

Arturo's still watching me, though. Whatever he sees, I try to hide it.

"You're not broken up over that girl of yours, are you? The one who's with Emilio now?"

"Nah," I say immediately.

Even if I were, I wouldn't let it show.

Don Pachino warned me: no bullshit with Emilio. Guess I know who ranks higher these days.

Emilio is his sister's kid. I'm just his *wife's* sister's kid.

Rocco slathers me with more shaving cream. The smell triggers all the old memories but none of the pleasure I used to feel sitting in this chair.

I'm a fucking ghost back to haunt his former life. I can't actually touch it. Can't actually taste it. Definitely can't feel a goddamn thing. My life's turned to shades of grey. Or maybe it's still in color but with one of those grainy filters that makes the images dull and cold.

Rocco moves the razor across my skin expertly. I wish Arturo hadn't brought it up because now all I can think about is how easy it would be for him to slice my jugular.

Would he do it? I used to be so secure in my bond with *La Famiglia*. The guys in this room could be trusted with my life. We were loyal to each other, to the Outfit. Everyone else, we locked out.

Now I don't trust any of them. And Rocco's not in the family. He's just an Italian small business owner who benefits from our patronage. He might hate all our guts. I used to think he treated us like royalty because he loved having us here. He liked the tips and the business. But who knows? Maybe he's just scared like everybody else.

Maybe he's collecting information, waiting for a moment to rat us all out.

Or maybe I'm in a paranoid mind-fuck I need to escape from.

The shave ends, and I view my image in the mirror. My jaw is smooth, but I look like a fucking corpse. Stone-faced. Dead eyes. Rotted out heart.

I stand and pay.

Arturo calls out when I head straight for the door. "You're not gonna hang around? What? You got something better to do?"

"Damn straight. He's gotta find a girl to exercise that dick of his," Angel chortles.

"Yeah," I agree. "That."

Marco and Leo watch me, seeing more than I wanna show. "You don't need a ride?" Marco asks. He drove me here.

"Nah, I'm good." I just want to be alone. Get the hell outta here. I lift my hand to them all and walk out.

Fanculo, that was painful. Even the simplest acts of living are like kneeling on sand now.

I gotta figure out how to wake the fuck up.

Chapter Six

Armando

I walk out of Rocco's.

It feels foreign to be able to do so. To be able to simply walk outside and breathe in fresh air of my own free will. No prison guard standing nearby while I enjoy my scheduled yard time. No fencing and barbed wire. Nothing but pure freedom.

It's a strange sensation. After so many years of confinement, the wide-open world has become like another planet. It's like I'm a stranger in a foreign land, with no idea of where to go or what to do now that I'm free. Surrounded by bustling people, their conversations and laughter filling the air, it all seems almost out of body.

"Hey," I hear Marco's voice from behind me.

I glance over my shoulder and see Marco and Leo following me out the door.

"I'm fine. Really," I say, actually meaning what I said that I want to be alone.

"I know you're going through shit," Leo begins, "But

Arturo is right. You're going to rebuild your life. It will start feeling like normal soon."

Marco places his hand on my shoulder. "Let's go get a drink or something."

"Nah, I know you guys have work to do today. I'm not a charity case." I take the time to look each of my cousins in the eyes. "I'm fine. I just need to go for a walk and get my shit in order. I appreciate it though."

I can tell by the way they both side eye each other that they don't want to leave me, but I'm right in the fact that they do need to get to work. *La Famiglia* is calling.

"Fine," Marco finally says. "But later. Drinks on me."

I nod and watch them both hop into Leo's car without another word. Grateful that they didn't put up too much of a fight, I decide to get out of the line of fire of Rocco's. I don't want another person to come out and feel pity for me and feel like they need to entertain me or something, so I begin to walk.

I know this neighborhood so well. Rocco's and then the florist, *Garden of Eden*, next door used to be part of my usual routine. A shave and then buy flowers for Grace. It was a comfortable routine. And now that I just had my shave, I realize I have no reason to walk next door to the florist. Who would I buy flowers for now?

Shaking my head, I know I need to give up this fucking pity party. I'm a free man. I should stop moping around. But the shackles of my past still cling to my wrists and ankles, dragging on my limbs. It's hard for me to feel happy or optimistic about the future when I am constantly reminded of the darkness of my past.

There's coldness inside, and I doubt it will be replaced with warmth.

And that's when something living surges in me—something primitive and instinctual. If I were a caveman, I'd raise my fucking spear. Because the guy in a grey sweatshirt leaning against the building moves in my direction. His hand reaches into his pocket.

I reach behind me before I remember I don't have a piece. It's illegal for a felon to carry, and I'm trying to keep my nose clean.

I'm instantly reminded of when I was jumped back in prison. Able to fight only with what little prison resources I had. Survival at all costs but nothing to rely on other than wit and brawn.

It all happens in a matter of seconds. I bum-rush the asshole, grabbing his wrist before he can point the pistol. The force of my attack launches us both off the stoop and into the gutter. My shoulder rams into the place where his collarbones meet, sending an explosion of pain across my chest.

We're tangled in a mess of limbs, struggling against each other as I try to get ahold of the weapon. He's stronger than I am; his face is twisted in a snarl.

Prison has dulled some of my physical prowess. I'm no longer the sharp knife I once was. My reflexes are faster, but my body isn't fine-tuned.

The guy is clearly out for blood, but I'm ready to fight to the death because I know if he gets that pistol free, I'm a dead man.

The struggle intensifies, and I feel my strength waning. He pries my grip from his wrist, and the gun creeps closer to his own hand. I know I'm outmatched. I'm not strong enough—not fast enough. I already feel the cold, hard steel of the gun against my skin. But I don't let go. I know that this is a fight for my life, and I won't back down. I twist his wrist, forcing him to drop the gun, and then I press my knee into his throat, so he can't scream for help.

I see the fear in his eyes as he struggles to break free from my grip, realizing I now have the upper hand. There's a moment of stillness as we stare each other down, and I feel the tension between us. It's a fight for dominance, for power, for our very lives. We are two predators in the wild, locked in a deadly battle.

The momentary pause on my behalf gives the man just enough time to free himself and attack me again with even more force, pushing us both against the doorway of the closest building, where we topple into the door of the florist. I use it, opening the door to trap his wrist and slamming it closed to dislodge the gun.

The weapon clatters to the floor inside the flower shop, and we both follow the movement. It's a mad scramble as we thrust the door open and tumble through. I land on the gun first.

I have to squelch my desire to shoot him point blank in the head.

I'm not going back to prison. Besides, I need to know who he's working for.

Because this is obviously a hit.

I empty the chamber of ammo and use the gun to smack him in the temple. He stumbles back but doesn't black out. Instead, he tackles me to the floor, and the gun goes sliding again.

Chapter Seven

Hannah

It's him. *Armando*. The one I used to lust after. This is not how I envisioned him reentering my store.

The scream gets stuck in my throat the moment reality sets in on what is actually happening before me. I'm too shocked to even move. For five long seconds, I just stand here like an idiot staring at the brutal fight.

Then I realize—I should do something.

Call someone.

I pick up my phone, not taking my eyes off the two men struggling on the floor. Both appear to be fighting for their lives. Armando is efficient and calm. He doesn't make a sound as he grapples with the other guy, rolling until he gets on top. Pummeling him into the ground. But then he loses his advantage and gets knocked backward into a shelf of plants.

I cover my mouth to keep in the cry of dismay at seeing my sweet inventory mauled. It's not like I have the money to replace even a single pot if they break one.

Armando catches sight of me. "End the call," he grits as he wrestles the guy to the floor in a headlock. The command in his voice is deadly. Scary enough to make me drop my phone to the counter with a clatter.

"I said *end it,*" he snarls. They're on the floor still, a writhing mass. This is not the nice man I remember who came into the store to buy flowers for his woman. This is a beast before me.

"I never dialed!" I protest, picking the phone up to flash him the screen.

He's not watching because the other guy produced a pocket knife. Armando narrowly misses getting sliced. There's a practiced precision to his movements like instead of being a mobster, he's actually a secret agent, a James Bond style superspy. Maybe it's the total lack of panic. He doesn't appear to be a man fighting for his life. He comes at his opponent like some angel of death sent to finish this guy.

Armando punches him hard in the face, follows to punch him again. The guy slashes with the knife at the same time, causing Armando to skirt to the side. Plants clatter from the table, pots crashing.

I whimper my dismay.

Armando picks one up and smashes it over the guy's head. The guy goes down, and Armando follows, his fingers around the guy's throat with one hand while he holds down the knife-wielding arm with the other. "Who sent you?" he demands.

The guy makes a gurgling sound but gets his arm away.

I scream when he stabs in the direction of Armando's face. Armando shifts in time but loses his advantage. The other guy scrambles up and smashes a pot from my metal plant stand into Armando's temple. He goes down hard, the crack of his skull against my tile floor making me cry out again.

I dial 9-1-1 on the phone but forget to press send because the guy launches himself at Armando with the knife.

In a gasp-worthy move, Armando somehow makes it back up just in time, swinging the heavy metal plant stand at the guy's head. The guy goes down hard and stays there.

In case you ever wondered, there's no mistaking death when you see it.

The shape his body takes is so completely askew. His neck is clearly broken.

Armando's hands tremble as he takes in the sight of the man lying motionless before him. I feel a chill go down my spine as shock paralyzes me in place.

Armando looks around the room, as if expecting to see more enemies coming for him, and I do the same.

What's coming next? What was that? What the fuck was that?

This can't be happening. Is this really happening?

Is there a bloody man lying dead in the middle of my florist shop?

The room is silent but for the sound of a ticking clock and the ringing in my ears.

Armando curses and drops to his knees, checking the guy's pulse.

Then he moves quickly—all efficiency and practice. He locks my door, closes the blinds and turns the sign to closed. He picks up the gun then drags the body past the counter toward the back. "Don't move," he tells me as he passes.

Don't move.

I don't know why, but until that moment, I hadn't considered *my* life might be in danger.

I was an observer, and I was rooting for one side to win.

My pick won the round.

But now it sets in that we're not going to be slapping high fives here. A guy *just got killed* in my shop, and I witnessed it.

I'm the *only* witness.

And the killer told me not to move. Which means I should definitely move.

Armando drags the body into my cooler. He's going to come out here and deal with me next.

That's a problem. I grab my purse and quietly, quickly walk past the cooler.

I sense Armando near, but I don't stop. I know if I do, it will be my last mistake. My heart pounds, and I can feel the sweat on my palms. I'm almost halfway to freedom when I hear a noise from the back of the shop. I spin to see Armando walking slowly towards me, gun in hand and a menacing look on his face. He's not going to let me go this easily. He takes a few more steps towards me, and I know I'm not going to make it out alive. I turn back towards the door, but it's too late. He's almost at me now, and there's no escape.

"Stop. I said don't fucking move!" That voice. He does command so well, every cell in my body wants to obey.

But that would be stupid, so I break into a run.

"Hannah."

Surprise that he remembered my name makes me falter. The hesitation costs me. He's on me in a flash, grabbing my elbow and whipping me around.

"I said, *don't move.*"

God, he's still devastatingly handsome. Square jaw. Aquiline nose. Hazel eyes with long lashes. He's so close, I smell the scent of Rocco's shaving cream on him. He's in a crisp, expensive blue button-down, open at the throat to reveal a clean white undershirt.

"I'm on your side," I say on exhale.

I'm not sure if it's self-preservation that makes me say the words or if it's the actual truth. I know Armando. I actually always liked the man... maybe a little too much.

I am on his side. I am.

He pivots me to face the wall, tugging one of my hands to pin there.

"I told you not to move." This is the voice of a mad man. Of the mafia. A killer. I need to remember that.

"I'm not going to say a thing." The famous last words of people before they are killed.

This is it. I'm dead.

I expect the knife to come to my throat. Instead, he smacks my ass.

I squeak in surprise. It was a hard smack—punitive, not playful—and for some reason, it turns me on.

I turn my head to look over my shoulder at him. An ass-smack isn't a real threat. It's something hot. Sexual. The cold in my veins evaporates.

He smacks my ass again, the other cheek this time.

Hello.

I don't have a clue what we're doing here, but I'm getting more excited than scared.

I must be confusing adrenaline for lust. Yes, that must be it.

Or is this insanity kicking in? Am I so terrified of dying that my body is confused by the foreign sensation, and—

He slaps my ass one more time, harder than the last.

My body responds. Warmth radiates from my core, and I can't help but moan in pleasure. It's embarrassing that I can't control emotions that I should keep hidden from him. I feel my heart racing, my skin tingling, and I'm growing wetter by the second.

He slides his hands down my sides, tracing a path of heat as he goes. He then grabs a roll of floral tape from my apron pocket. "Here's what's going to happen." He twists my arms behind my back and ties my wrists together with the floral tape. It's flexible, but he wraps it a dozen times and makes it tight, so I can't twist enough to get it off. "You're going to stay right here, facing this wall, until I get back. You're not going to move. You're not going to make a sound. *Capisce?*"

I nod my head quickly. "Yeah, okay." I sound breathless.

I'm scared. Scared shitless. But there's also something crazy churning inside me. Some spiraling heat, a tingling awareness.

I don't know if it's because I had a crush on this guy before or because he slapped my ass and woke up an erogenous area, but liquid heat pools between my legs.

He steps in front of me, and I feel his breath on my skin. He leans close and whispers in my ear. "Follow the rules, Flowers. Follow them or else." His voice is low, possessive. His hot breath tickles my skin, sending pleasure coursing through me.

He takes my chin in his hand and turns my face up to his. He pulls away slightly, and I gasp for breath, my heart thudding in my chest.

He traces his finger along my jaw and down my throat. "I'll be back soon. Don't move."

Armando then takes a step back and looks me up and down, his gaze burning with what I hope is desire. His eyes linger for a moment on the tightness of the floral tape binding my wrists, and then he gives a faint smirk. "Be a good girl," he warns, before turning and walking away.

Am I reading him wrong? And have I lost my fucking mind? I shouldn't be feeling anything but the overwhelming need to run and run fast. I should be fighting, screaming, and most definitely be terrified.

And yet, I stand here with my heart pounding and... my body on fire with desire. The heat between my legs grows stronger with each passing second, and a strange thrill of excitement shoots through me.

My body aches with anticipation. I'm still bound and helpless, but this time my fear has been replaced by something else. Something exciting. I can't help but wonder— maybe even fantasize—what will happen when Armando returns.

I listen as he steps back into my cooler. I hear the sound of his voice speaking in short, clipped sentences. He must be on the phone.

Who is he talking to?

What is he saying?

Oh Jesus, is he calling more of the mafia to come and help him with this... *situation*? Is Garden of Eden about to become even more of a blood bath than it already is but with my blood?

If I were smart, I wouldn't stick around to figure out what he's going to do with me. I'd somehow find a way to escape. I'm not the stupid girl who falls for the bad boy. I've never been weak. I've never been the damsel in distress. So why in the hell am I even standing here?

And just as I'm starting to think about inching toward the back door, he returns and spins me around. With my wrists bound behind my back, my double D's thrust forward and spread. "All right, Flowers. What am I going to do with you?"

Maybe it's self-preservation. Maybe it's the crush. Or

the way my ass still tingles where he slapped it, but I do the only thing I can think of, which is to lean forward and kiss his mouth.

His lips press against mine, stealing my breath away. His tongue slips inside, coaxing mine into a slow, dizzying dance. I moan into his mouth, my hips shifting against his mass, like some new north star.

Armando's hands slide lower, over my hips and down my thighs. His fingers brush against the fabric of my clothes, and I shudder. He cups my ass in his hands, kneading and squeezing, sending fire into every nerve ending. This kiss...

Chapter Eight

rmando

A I rear back from the kiss in surprise. It's unexpected and juicy and Fahrenheit 451-level hot.

And just like defib paddles applied to my chest, a jolt of energy surges through me.

The lights come on. My body comes back to life.

It's been almost five years since I've tasted a woman, and there's suddenly so much lost time to make up for.

I'm on her in a second, kissing the fuck out of that lush mouth, sliding one hand up her shirt. I just killed a guy and hid the body in Flower's freezer. That's what I should be dealing with. But the moment she kissed me, color bled back into my world. I need to explore it like I need my next breath. She's in a short skirt, and I'm suddenly way up it with my other hand, cupping her pussy.

The soft silky fabric of her panties is damp.

That's all the information my brain needs to go full steam ahead. I'm an animal, incapable of pulling back. Raw instinct propels my actions more than any coherent thought.

I shove her shirt up and lower my head to feast on her

nipple, her gasps filling my ears. "Tell me, Flowers." I slide my fingers under the gusset of her panties to drag through her damp folds. "What got you so wet?" I screw one finger into her, and she gasps and goes up on her toes.

My body is on fire, my need so sharp I can taste it. I'm going to take her right here, until all the darkness inside of me has been driven out. Until I can breathe again.

Her head falls back as I thrust my finger deeper, stealing a moan from her parted lips. Whether she wants to or not, she grinds her hips, pushing down onto my hand. I'm buried so deep inside of her, I'm touching her core.

"Please," she whispers.

Is she begging for me to continue, or for me to free her and walk out that door? The line between right and wrong is too blurred for me to know.

My heart pounds in my ears, and my cock feels like steel. Our mouths crash together in a desperate kiss, exploring, tasting, teasing. My free hand curls around her body as I tease her lips with my tongue. I feel her tremble beneath me as I press another finger into her pussy.

Her fervent whimpers drive me on until I'm so hard, so ready to devour every inch of her that I'm trembling like a weak man. My hand snakes up to cup the back of her neck as we breathe each other in. The heat from our bodies entwining is almost too much for me to take.

If she begged and pleaded for me to stop, there'd be no way I could.

I know she can't be comfortable pressed up against the wall with her hands bound behind her back, but I can't seem to dial back my attention.

Yes, there is a dead man in her cooler, and I have her here as my captive.

But the world around us seems to disappear, leaving

only us two enclosed by sexual heat and frenzied desire. Nothing else matters except this moment when she is all mine.

And that's what she is. *Mine.*

As adrenaline from my fight flows through my body, I can't control the demon from coming out and claiming her fully.

I scissor my fingers, spreading her tight little hole, driving them inside harder and faster, pounding into her with an intensity that has her gasping for air as her body quivers beneath me. I don't stop until I feel her muscles clenching around me as she cries out in pleasure.

"You like being tied up? Or was it your spanking?" I ask.

She stares at me with gold-flecked brown eyes. Her wild mane of curls tumble all around her head like a halo, falling over her right eye. She's gorgeous—pure femininity embodied in a small, curvy, dark-skinned package. I haven't been with a Black woman before, but after living with guys of every color in prison, the racism I grew up around has long since disappeared from my thoughts. But even more importantly, I've never been with a more beautiful woman. Breathtaking would be an understatement. A true goddess who can't be matched by another.

"Or was it—" I frown, remembering the shit show I'm in. "Was it the violence—what you saw out there? What had you moaning out my name, Flowers? What has this pussy so wet? Does death turn you on?"

"I-I don't know."

For a moment, my rational brain tries to break in. Slow my roll. Remind me that this isn't the time or the place. But her pussy clenching around my fingers and the flush in her cheeks brings me back to the only thing I care about—seeing this thing through.

"You need me to alleviate the ache down here?"

I stop moving, waiting for her consent. We're both breathing hard, our faces just an inch apart. She holds my gaze and gives a tiny nod, just before she attacks me with another kiss.

I go nuts on her.

I've never had a female as the aggressor before, and it fucking drives me wild. I shove my fingers deep inside her again and squeeze her ass with my other hand. She moans and whimpers her pleasure, squirming against me, her lips still pulling on mine, tongue lashing into my mouth.

I screw a third finger inside her, prepping her for what's to come. I don't mean to be so raw and dirty, but my body moves of its own accord. My other hand strokes between her ass cheeks, seeking the tight bud of her anus.

She cries out in surprise when I find it, contracting and falling against me.

I push her back against the wall and finger-fuck her with my left hand while my right alternates between rubbing her anus and squeezing her plump asscheeks.

Her pink Converse shuffle and dance beneath her. My dick isn't even out, but I experience her pleasure as my own. It's been a long time, but I don't remember ever having a girl go off like this. Not so easy. Not so fast. Never so welcoming. The mixture of eroticism and tension between us makes it seem like my life depends on getting her off.

But maybe that's the adrenaline from almost getting killed.

From—

But I'm not thinking about that now. Right now, I'm watching Hannah, the beautiful young florist, fly over the crest of her orgasm.

She screams when it hits hard, and I smother her mouth with mine, swallowing her cries.

I keep my body pressed against hers and slow-pump my fingers until her channel stops milking them. "Fuck, Flowers." I ease my fingers out, then hold her gaze with heavy lids as I put them in my mouth. "Tastes like heaven." My voice sounds guttural and rough. "I could spend all night eating your pussy."

She blinks at me, her eyes unfocused and glassy, her cheeks flushed with color.

I remembered her as gorgeous, but she was so young when I went away. Barely out of high school. Now she's all grown up. She pierced her nose. Grew her hair out into wild, golden-tipped ringlets that fall nearly to her ass. She's gloriously beautiful.

I can't help myself. I need more. Like I'm going to fucking die on this spot if I don't get my dick wet *right now*.

"I want to be inside you," I find myself saying out loud. It's wrong. So wrong. I have the girl tied up with florist tape, for fuck's sake. But something about the way she looks at me makes me think I have a chance. "You gonna let me bend you over that counter and fuck that sweet pussy hard?"

Christ. I'm so fucking depraved. What girl would say yes to that?

But unbelievably, she wets her lips and says, "Do you have a condom?"

Fuck, yeah, I have a condom. I may not have had the urge to use one until now, but I sure as hell prepared for the opportunity in case I did.

I have her bent over in said position in about two seconds flat. I shove her short skirt up and slap her ass cheeks again several times, then yank down her panties. I love the pink blush on her ass, my handprints starting to show.

I find the condom. The pistol I'd stowed in my waist-band falls to the floor when I release my cock, but I ignore it, too blinded with desire to even think straight.

Somehow, I get the condom on.

Drag my cock through her juices.

She's still wonderfully wet. Gloriously, miraculously wet. I sink into her heat, and my entire body shudders with pleasure.

"Fuck. You feel so good." I'm not chatty, but one touch from this girl, and I'm babbling like a brook. I have her face pressed down on the workbench, her glorious dark brown and honey-colored curls spread in a wild curtain. I push it back from her face, then gather a fistful at the back of her head. "You like having your hair pulled?"

She makes a little whimpering sound like, "Uhn." Might be a no, but her pussy gushes with fresh lubricant, so I take it as a yes.

I take a firmer grip on her hair and begin to thrust in time with her pants of pleasure. I can feel every twitch and spasm of her pussy as I push my way deeper into her depths. Her body shakes as if electric currents are coursing through her. I quicken my pace, driving harder into her with each thrust.

I reach down to caress her breasts, kneading and massaging them as I continue to drive relentlessly into her. Her moans become more intense as I reach around to stroke and tease her clit. I feel her tightening around me, pushing me closer and closer to the edge. As she shudders and cries out in pleasure, I thrust as deep as I can.

And then I lose all control. I fuck her fast and hard. Fireworks dance before my eyes. My body explodes into pleasure. Heat spikes at the base of my spine. My blood sizzles.

I've been dead for years. Who knew all I needed was a good fuck to come back to life? And it is the *best* of fucks.

Nothing compares. Every stroke I take inside her makes me jerk with pleasure. I'm riding her too hard, but I can't dial it back. My loins slap against her ass. Her bound wrists bounce on her lower back.

"My hips," she gasps. "It hurts."

Oh shit. I'm banging them against the hard wooden workbench.

I wrap my arm around the front of her to provide padding, and then keep slamming the hell out of her. I don't give a shit that I'm bruising my arm. In fact, I sort of relish the sensation. Pleasure and pain mingle together into a symphony of sensory feedback. Her scent gets up in my nostrils, along with the smell of roses and lilies and whatever other flowers she has in the place.

She gasps as I drive hard and deeper, feeling the pressure inside her building to an unbearable degree. Her hips begin to quiver in response, begging for more. I reach down and slide one hand between us, my fingers finding her clit and rubbing in circles. She moans as she arches her back and grinds against me, her body shaking and writhing. My thrusts become faster and more powerful as I drive toward the edge.

I'm too far gone to wait for her to come, definitely too lost to figure out how to make her orgasm. I mutter a curse and shove deep, pulling her head and torso back up against the front of me as I finish.

I bite her ear, flick it with my tongue. "I'm sorry I hurt you," I murmur against the soft skin of her jaw.

She whimpers slightly, and a pang of regret wavers through me.

Funny.

I just ended a guy on her floor and felt nothing. I was the Terminator doing a job. Now I suddenly have a conscience. And I *should* be sorry. I just fucked a girl I trussed like a chicken and took as my prisoner. And her asking if I had a condom probably did not constitute consent. It was a plea for some measure of safety.

Fuck. What kind of *stronzo* am I?

Chapter Nine

*H*annah

Oh my *gawd*.

I'm dizzy, my body buzzes. I'd forgotten to be afraid while we were having sex, but now, awareness creeps back. I'm pinned against my workbench with my panties down and my wrists tied behind my back, a semi-stranger's cock still stretching me.

What in the hell am I doing?

It may not seem like it now, but I'm usually cautious about who I have sex with.

I don't know how I lost my head like that. It was just so hot. So animalistic. Feral. That teenage crush on Armando made it feel so necessary. I didn't come, but I was so close.

Now I'm tingling and hot and needy as hell. Which doesn't help the tolling bells for foreboding.

I could be in real trouble here. Life or death stuff.

I'm sorry I hurt you.

I cling to that one piece of evidence that this man is not a psychopath. That he didn't just rape me. That I'm going to walk out of here alive.

A knock pounds on my back door, and Armando pulls out of me with a curse. He yanks my panties up and drops the condom in the wastebasket.

The taut urgency returns to his movements as he spins me around, his gaze darting around the premises. I stiffen when he pulls a roll of duct tape from my shelf and rips off a small piece.

"No—"

He slaps it over my mouth.

I scream behind the tape, terror suddenly ripping through me.

Ohmygodohmygodohmygod.

What's happening? What's he going to do with me?

The knock sounds again, and Armando grabs my arm, propelling me toward the storage closet.

"Shh." He puts his finger over my taped lips as he pushes me backward into the crowded dark space.

I try to scream *no*, but it comes out as nothing more than a muffled sound.

"Quiet, Hannah." There's a warning to his tone.

The door shuts.

Panic sets in. I'm afraid of the dark. I don't like small spaces. And I definitely don't want to be tied up and left in here to rot.

I want to slam my head against the door to make noise, except he was expecting whomever showed up at my back door. So it's someone he knows.

Which means I can't hope for a rescue from them.

In fact, if he's hiding me in here from his associates out there, it could be for my own safety. Like they might insist on killing me.

Oh fuck.

My entire body starts to shake. Not a slight tremble, but

54

a terrible shuddering that makes my knees knock together and my ribs lock down in a painful cinching.

I hear male voices and footsteps tromping past the closet. The sound of a body being dragged.

Tears drip down my cheeks and over the duct tape on my mouth. My breath rasps harshly in and out of my nose.

"What about the florist?" a male asks just outside the closet. "Need me to clean that up?"

"I got rid of her," Armando says.

"Yeah?"

"Yeah. She didn't see anything. It's cool."

I was right. He's protecting me. That's why I'm in the closet. Because if his buddies out there knew I saw something, I might have to die.

But then... how do I know he's not going to kill me anyway? Maybe he just wants to make me his fuck toy first. Keep me tied up in his closet for months and months and *then* throw me dead in a ditch.

Oh my God.

This is bad.

"I'll finish the clean up here. I owe you. Don't tell anyone about this. I'll tell the don myself, yeah?"

"Yeah, as long as you do."

"Swear to Christ. Hey—get rid of his gun, too. I can't carry one."

"Are you fucking nuts? Someone's trying to kill you. You need a piece."

"I can take care of myself."

He definitely can. I just saw him take care of an armed man without ever firing. In fact, he'd purposely emptied the gun chamber. I don't think he meant to kill that guy at all. It was definitely self-defense.

"I fucking hope so."

The back door shuts. I wait, my shaking intensifying as the possibilities fly through my mind.

What's happeningwhat's shappeningwhat's shappening?

The closet door flies open, and I blink at the sudden light. Armando's face comes into focus. His brows lower when he looks at me. "Aw, baby. Did you think I was going to leave you in here?" He thumbs away the tears under my left eye.

Did I? Not really. I just didn't like being tied up and standing in a dark closet. Feeling helpless.

He drags me forward, out of the closet and works the corner of tape free over my upper lip. "I'm sorry for this." He yanks it all off in one pull. A strangled cry erupts as the tape leaves my lips.

"You okay?"

"No," I snap. "Let me go." My demand sounds way more watery than firm.

"Sorry, Flowers. That's not possible." He pulls me into my workshop. "Here's what's going to happen. I'm going to clean up your shop, and you're going to stay where I put you and not make a sound. Can you do that, or do I need to put you back in the closet?"

I'm tempted—so tempted—to knee him in the balls. Except I just saw what this man is capable of. He fought a man armed with a gun *and* a knife, and he won. There's no way it would go well for me.

He thumbs away the tears under my right eye. "Be cool, Flowers, and we won't have any problems. Okay?"

"I don't want you here." It's a dumb thing to say, but it's true. I want him to leave. I want him out of my shop. My life. My reality.

I think I'm going to puke.

I wish this evening never happened.

"Feeling's mutual, Flowers." He pulls back the stool at my desk, which is essentially in the hallway where he can see me from the front room and pushes me into it.

"It's Hannah." I turn to face him as he gets a broom and dustpan out of the closet and moves swiftly into the shop. "But you know that."

I'm a little bitter that his speaking my name was my downfall. If I hadn't hesitated when he called my name, I would've made it out the back door.

"Hannah." His back is to me. He sweeps up the broken pots and soil with swift, deft movements. "You own the place now."

I watch the muscles in his back ripple each sure stroke of the broom. I shouldn't be flattered that he knows things about me. And really, it's not like he knows something earth-shattering. It's a basic fact everyone in his organization knows. Yet it makes my pulse quicken.

"Armando."

The sound of his name makes his head snap up and brings his gaze to mine. My stomach drops away. He's as breathtaking as I remembered him, except so very serious now. There's no hint of a smile on his face anymore. None of the charm and ease. And the eyes...

Compassion weasels in.

Because his eyes look ancient.

"You remembered."

I shrug like he never starred in a hundred of my darkest fantasies. "You remembered mine, too. Where have you been?" My voice sounds rusty.

Shutters close behind his eyes, and he turns back to his work. "Prison. Just out."

A shiver runs through me. *Prison.* Josie and I didn't think of that possibility.

"Was that your... first time since getting out?" It would explain why he was an animal when I kissed him.

At first, I think he's not going to answer. He ignores me, dumping the contents of the dustpan into the garbage. Then he mutters, "Yeah."

I'm simultaneously pleased and destroyed by that. I guess I wanted to believe he was just that attracted to me. I mean, he did remember my name.

I am such a fool.

Then I realize he's watching me, and I try to school my face. Keep on a blank mask like he wears.

"You okay? I was... rough."

Oh shit, I'm blushing. I sense the heat crawl up my neck and spread to my ears and cheeks.

He *was* rough. And it was hot. I never knew I'd like having my hair pulled or my butt slapped, but I did. I'm still needy for more like a glutton. Almost painfully needy.

"I'd buy you flowers, but I'm guessing that's not your thing." He gives me the barest hint of a smile, and stupid me, I reward him with one in return.

"Only if you get them here," I say, which is dumb because I wouldn't really want a guy to buy flowers from me to give to me. I only said it because I need the money so badly, I'd be offended if he shopped anywhere else.

And why in the hell am I even examining this line of thought? I'm being held captive in my own shop. *By a murderer.*

It's not time for roses and romance.

So I poke. "What happened to the fiancée?"

He grimaces, his expression going harder. "Lotta questions, Flowers."

I arrange the pieces of the puzzle in my mind. "She didn't wait," I answer for him.

He straightens the toppled table and rearranges the remaining plants on it.

"I'm sorry." It slips out before I can bite back my offering of compassion.

He ignores my sympathy, walking past me to fill the mop bucket in my large utility sink. I smell the scent of bleach. Well, at least he cleans up his own mess. He could've ordered me to do it.

I twist my hands behind my back. "These hurt."

"Stop moving."

"Thanks. Great suggestion. I hadn't thought of that."

He cuts a look at me while he dumps a generous helping of bleach in with the water. "You're tied up because you gave me trouble. Maybe rethink the attitude if you want me to let out the leash."

"Leash?"

He wheels the mop bucket into the shop. There was a smattering of blood on the floor, but not much, thankfully. He swabs the entire floor.

"Why didn't you use the gun? Too loud?"

He shakes his head. "Shut up, Flowers."

"You didn't want him dead."

Armando makes a tsking sound as he mops the hall, then wheels past me and dumps the dirty water into the sink. "Keep out of this. You saw nothing. If anyone asks, there was a struggle, but we both left to finish things outside. You locked the place up and left early."

My stool is a spinning one, and I use my feet to whirl around on it like a kid. "No offense, but that story would not hold up under questioning."

Armando stalks over to me.

The part of me bold enough to talk back shrivels, especially when I remember this man is a brutal killer.

59

He stops when he reaches me, indecision flickering in his expression. Maybe he sees the fear on my face. He reaches for me, and I flinch. He slows his touch. Burrows his fingers through my hair at the side of my head then curls them up to tug it tight.

"Listen. Hannah. I'd rather not say the shit I'm supposed to say right now. Not to you."

My stomach flip flops as I try to decode the meaning of his words. I keep getting caught on the *not to you.*

Like he *does* think I'm something special. But maybe, I'm looking too hard for meaning, so I won't regret what I just let him do to me.

Like I want to believe that crazy rough sex meant something to him.

I know I still feel it all over. And if I stop looking for meaning or wondering if I just degraded myself, I might believe experiencing a man like Armando was worth it. I'm pretty sure he just ruined me for vanilla sex. Ruined me for kinder, gentler men. I should've known there was a reason those mafia assholes always appealed to me. I prefer an alpha male. I'm sure it's a purely biological weakness many women share with me.

I try to swallow around the invisible band choking me.

"I won't tell anyone what I saw," I manage to say. My voice sounds strained.

"Good girl. Then we won't have any problems."

Oh, we'll still have problems. Individually and together.

I screw up my courage because making demands isn't my strong suit, especially not in a crazy situation like this. I lift my chin. "But you're paying for the damages here." I don't take my gaze off his face as I flutter my hand in the direction where the pots had been broken.

"Yeah. Of course."

Whew. That was easier than expected.

I sit forward on the stool, as much as I can with his grip on my hair holding me immobile. It only has the effect of pushing my tits out. His gaze drops to my cleavage and hunger creeps into his expression.

I lick my lips, and his gaze lifts to my mouth. "A-are you going to let me go?"

The hunger drops away, replaced by that hardened mask he wears. "We'll see, Flowers." He releases my hair and turns away.

A chill creeps across my skin.

All the horrific doubts crowd into my brain and cut off intelligent thought.

I surge to my feet. He whirls, his hand around my throat in seconds, not squeezing, but guiding me back to my seat. His voice is even when he shakes his head and says, "I didn't say you could move."

And it's that cold hardness more than anything that freaks me the hell out.

He must see the panic in my expression because he puts his finger lightly over my lips, trailing it downward. "Shh. Take it easy. You do what I say, you won't get hurt. *Capisce?*"

I stare back at him and nod quickly.

"Good girl."

Chapter Ten

Armando
    Fuck.
    I don't know what I'm going to do with the girl. I can't keep her tied up forever.

She is a witness to a murder, but I don't harm the innocent.

That guy I killed today? He was a professional. Not a good one but definitely a guy who took money for the hit. Probably sent by the Hermanos.

Cazzo.

I went straight from my first confession out of the joint back to hell. Don Pachino told me to keep my nose clean. What a fucking laugh. I finish wiping the shop, trying to erase all evidence of the struggle. I owe her for a couple pots, but the damage isn't too bad. Luckily, there wasn't much blood.

Marco is a prince for taking care of the body for me. He's the only guy I trusted enough to call. There are soldiers. I used to have my own crew, and I coulda called one of them, but something told me not to.

I stand in front of Hannah and slide my palm around the meat of her arm to lift her to her feet. She glares up at me.

"Where are the keys to that van out back?"

Her eyes widen. "Why? You can't put a body in it—"

"There's no body," I cut her off. "But we need to leave—now. And I don't have a car."

I don't have a license, either, but that's sort of the least of my problems. I probably should've kept that gun, too. At this point, I'm in for murder and kidnapping. The five years for a felon in possession of a firearm is minor in comparison.

"I-it's a piece of shit. I don't even use it because half the time it stalls on me."

Fuck.

"I'll take the risk. *Where are the goddamn keys?*"

"In my purse—*Jesus.*" She lifts her chin toward the purse tucked under the counter.

I like that she's offended by my tone and gives a little shit back to me. It means she's not scared out of her mind. She still believes I ought to treat her better, which, of course, is true. I'm just out of fucking practice with having manners.

I rifle through her purse and find the keys then check her driver's license for an address. "You live alone?"

She pales. "W-why?"

"'Cause someone's trying to kill me. I don't think I should bring you to my place. Is your place cool?"

Relief flickers over her face, and she gives me a shaky nod. "Yeah. I live alone. I mean, it's small."

"Yeah, I just got out of a seven by twelve foot cell. I think we're good."

She gets more words out of me than I've spared for anyone since I got out, my mother and Don Pachino included. I tug her to the door, but she balks, looking back toward the register.

I tried to read her resistance. "You don't leave cash in the register at night?"

"I need to make a deposit—tonight. Or your boss won't get his money when he cashes my check." A sheen of tears fills her eyes, and it does something weird to my chest.

I've felt nothing since they locked me up.

Nada.

No heart beating in my fucking chest.

But now empathy suddenly rears its pansy head.

I don't know. I guess I'm surprised how little she's fussed over my treatment of her, but here she's tearing up about the money.

She must be in dire financial straits.

Buying the business might have been a shit move for her.

I bring her back to the register and flip through the keys on her ring until I find the small one that fits. There's not that much money in it. I'd say less than three hundred bucks.

"There's an envelope in that drawer." She indicates it with her chin.

I find the zippered pouch and tuck the money inside. "That it?"

The sheen of tears appears again, and she nods.

Definitely money trouble.

Well, if she keeps my secret, I'll owe her. I shove my hand in my pocket. "How short are you?"

"What?" She searches my face in surprise. "Oh, um, at least a hundred, maybe more."

I flip through my cash the don set me up with when I renewed my oaths to him and the Outfit, or as the don likes to call it, *la Cosa Nostra*. I shove another six hundred in her money pouch. "That cover it?"

Her eyes round, and she nods, breath erratic.

"Good. Here's what's going to happen. You play it cool —real cool—and I'll untie you and let you ride up front in the passenger seat. We'll make your deposit." I smack her ass with the money pouch. "Then we'll go to your place. *Capisce?*"

She nods quickly. "I'll be cool. I promise."

When she licks her lips, I'm overcome with the sudden urge to claim that mouth again. Because I have never kissed a girl like I just kissed her. So full of passion and heat and raw desperate need. I want to get another taste.

And then I want to see those lips stretched around my cock. Working my length with the same receptivity she showed me bent over her workbench earlier. I want to see the pleasure in her eyes when I make her come, feel her body tremble and shake with a pleasure that only I can give her. I move closer to her, my hands sliding up her arms as I press my hips against hers, not leaving any room for doubts as to what I want or where I want it.

I swear to Christ, she must read my thoughts because when I look down, I see her nipples protruding beneath her layers.

And I've lost my mind because all I can think is maybe I should fuck her again before we leave.

Instead, I tug her toward the back and out the door to the alley where Marco and I loaded the body into his trunk forty-five minutes ago. I stop at the back door and use the teeth of one of her keys to rip the tape off her wrists.

Before I release her, I wrap my hand in her hair and tug her head back. "Don't make me sorry, Hannah." My body's right up against hers. Her chest rises and falls rapidly, drawing my gaze to her delectable cleavage. I trace my thumb across the line of her jaw.

"I won't. I'll be cool. Promise."

"Good girl." I release her in degrees, not wanting to separate my body from hers. Not sure I can trust her outside this shop. She could scream. Or run. Or grab for her phone.

But I guess this is how I find out. If she misbehaves, I'll deal with it. And then I'll know I can't trust her.

Which means...fuck, I don't want to think what that would mean because I don't hurt women. And I definitely don't hurt the innocent.

And she's both.

Chapter Eleven

Armando

A I open the back door and push her out then pull it shut behind us and test the lock. "Show me you can be trusted." I smack her ass again.

I'm not usually the ass-smacking type. At least I wasn't before prison. Sure, I gave my fiancée a spank or two during sex, but Hannah is a different story altogether.

Her ass is juicy. Round, plump. Firm. I don't just want to bend her over and fuck her again, I want to spank her brown cheeks rosy and own that ass with my cock.

Jesus, fuck.

I'm a feral animal.

A wild beast rutting.

And Hannah is my prey.

I want to throw her in the back of the van and have another go at that lush body of hers right here, right now.

I almost wish she'd give me a reason to keep manhandling her, but she behaves herself, strutting straight to the passenger side of the beat up, rust-covered, 1970s Dodge Ram van with a flower decal on the side and waiting for me to unlock it. The paint of the aging van is peeling and chipping off, the rust eating at the edges. The lettering of *Garden of Eden Florists* on the side is blistered, peeled, faded and flaking, leaving yellow paint behind.

"Does this heap even run?" I say the words out loud as I open the door for her. I don't mean to shame the girl, but Jesus, this tin can is a dinosaur that has truly seen its day.

"Are you even allowed to drive?" she snarks back as she climbs in.

"No." I slam her door and walk around, keeping an eye on her through the windows. She sits down and folds her hands in her lap, perfectly behaved.

Almost too perfectly. Either she's more worried about getting this money in the bank than she is her safety with me, or she's planning something.

I hope it's the former.

I get in and start the van. Correction—*try* to start the van. It takes a couple attempts before it sputters to life. I don't know how the fuck she handles flower deliveries with a van that needs work. Which I guess speaks to her money problems.

The van smells of lilac and gasoline, and there is a large crack in the windshield. Though the engine is now running, it's not exactly humming like a well-oiled machine. It'll be a miracle if we even make it out of this alley.

I glance at her hands in her lap. Her wrists still wear the mark of the tape I bound them with, and there's an angry red scrape down her arm.

The fuck?

My hand shoots out to snatch up her wrist before I can dial back the aggression. I'm pissed at myself for hurting her. I don't even know when it happened. My body goes into full rage mode like I'm going to defend her against myself. The aggression is different from how I was back there with the hitman. Not so clean and clinical. There's emotion this time.

She gasps and tries to pull away. I force myself to gentle my hold because I'm scaring the hell out of her. "Did I do that?" I manage to choke, running my thumb over the long thick red line.

She looks at me like I've lost my mind.

Maybe I have.

"What? The scratch?" A shaky laugh tumbles from her lips. "No. My kitten did that last night. He fell in the bathtub while I was in it. Turns out, cats can fly." Another nervous laugh.

Kitten.

Kitten. It takes a moment for the word to even process. Cute furry thing with claws. Right. Her cat scratched her.

Not me.

I relax my hold and sit back in my seat, forcing myself to exhale. I want to ask if I hurt her, but I already know I did. The skin around her wrists and bruises on her hips. Hopefully nothing worse. Nothing deep and psychological that will haunt her for the rest of her life.

Yeah, right. Guy comes in, kills a man in front of her, then ties her up and fucks her. She's definitely scarred for life.

"My thighs are all scratched up, too."

My eyes drop to the hemline of her short skirt. Fuck if I don't want to see those scratches for myself now.

I wrench my gaze back to the windshield. I need to get my head back in the game. I dip my cock in a chick once, and suddenly everything's haywire for me.

Hannah's got some kind of magic pussy or something. Like that doesn't sound insane.

"Which bank?" I ask roughly. "They'd better have a drive-thru."

"Chicago City Bank on Lincoln. Um...hopefully." She sounds doubtful like she knows they don't but just isn't telling me.

"Do they or don't they, Flowers?" I snap.

She reaches over and touches my forearm. "Please? I *have* to make this deposit."

It's so fucked that I'm even considering this. She's my hostage until I figure out what the hell I'm going to do with her, and I'm going to go run her errands?

Give her at least a dozen opportunities to signal for help or run away?

On the other hand, the vague plan in the back of my head is to sit on her until I get a feel for her. Figure out if she's gonna squeal or not. Ignoring her needs isn't going to win trust. And since I seem reluctant to make the kind of threats that will keep her quiet out of fear, I'm probably gonna have to go on trust if I don't want to get rid of her.

And I definitely don't.

I grind my molars, trying to come to a decision. Stopping at the bank is a really, really bad one. I can't send her in alone. I can't leave her in the van unless I tie her up in the back, and doing that in public would be risky.

"Please."

I glance over and curse. "You try anything, Flowers, I will make you sorry."

That's the closest I can come to threatening her.

Would I hurt a woman? No fucking way. We may be criminals, but goodfellas swear an oath to respect women and our elders. I nearly punched myself in the face when I thought I'd scraped her arm.

Doesn't mean I wouldn't smack her ass and tie her up. Show her who's boss.

"I won't."

I growl but find a spot to park near the bank. "Don't open your fucking door until I come around." I glare at her.

She pales slightly. "Chill, Armando. I'm not going to try anything. I just have to deposit this money." She picks up the money pouch I set between our seats and waves it. Her hand's trembling like crazy, and I feel bad about scaring her, but I don't apologize. I just give her the hairy eyeball as I shut the door and stalk around to her side.

She waits until I open it, like I instructed.

"Good girl." I offer a hand to help her out.

She clutches the bag to her chest. "Can I get my purse? In case they need I.D.?"

I already pocketed her phone, but I still don't like it. I reach for the purse and pull the I.D. out of her wallet. "Let's go." I take her hand but fold it behind her back, like she's under arrest. It's symbolic—her other hand is free, but she'll get my meaning.

I start sweating the moment we walk inside the bank. The air is thick with the smell of polished wood, antiseptic, and body odor. There are people everywhere. A security guard by the door with a gun. He's a big, lumbering guy, with a mustache and an ill-fitting uniform. The eyes that look at you from behind his glasses are tired and bored.

All Hannah has to do is scream for help, and it's over.

"Armando," Hannah murmurs. I like it when she says my name. I like that she remembered me. She wriggles her hand in mine, and I realize I'm squeezing too tightly.

I loosen my grip slightly and pull her hand out from behind her back to swing between us. We walk up to the teller, and I swear to Christ my heart's beating so loud I think the teller will hear it. She'll probably think I'm trying to rob the bank and sound the silent alarm.

Hannah quickly fills out a deposit slip and pushes the cash across the counter.

"You had an overdraft charge today," the teller informs her.

Hannah tenses. "I did? I thought I had until the end of the day to make the deposit."

The teller looks at her screen. "No, it's real time. The check came through around two p.m."

Okay, so she wasn't playing me. She really does have money trouble. I tap the stack of cash with the deposit slip. "Will this cover it?"

The teller counts the money and types into her computer. "The overdraft charge was $35, so you're twenty-two short."

I shove my hand in my pocket to pull out another five hundred Benjamins. "Put that in the account, too."

She nods, counts it and types some more. "Will that be all?"

I close my fingers around Hannah's hand again. "Yes." I start to pull her away when the teller calls back to me.

"Hang on."

I freeze, a tight cord of tension running between my shoulder blades.

"Here's your receipt."

Jesus, I just want to get out of this place. But I turn and grab the receipt then pull my little captive with me.

"You were short by a lot," I say as we walk out of the building. Again, I'm not trying to shame her, I'm just wondering what the fuck her plan was.

She stiffens, tucking her curls behind her left ear.

"Better to be short with the bank than short with the don, right?"

"Yeah," I agree. "You behind on rent?"

I don't know why I'm worried for her now, but I am. If she owes Don Pachino money and doesn't pay it, he'll swallow her business up in a heartbeat. That flower shop will become a money-laundering machine. Every delivery van will be driven by a soldier on Family business between making the flower rounds. It's actually such a perfect setup, I'm surprised he hasn't already moved on it.

She shakes her head, sending her golden-tipped curls rippling like a waterfall, but there's still an ocean of worry in the set of her shoulders. I get it. She made the rent today, but she's still worried about tomorrow and the next day and the one after that.

I put her back in the van. Considering what a shit show today was, I'm somewhat amazed this stop actually turned out okay.

I drive to her neighborhood, which isn't that far from her shop in Little Italy. Parking is a bitch, so I circle around a half dozen times. I don't want to park too far from her place because it gives her a better chance to scream for help or run or... whatever.

The stupid thing is that I know exactly how to stop any hint of that behavior. I know how to issue threats. I've perfected mean and cruel.

I could easily make her piss herself with fear without ever laying a hand on her.

But I can't bring myself to do it. Even though it would make things simpler.

Make my job at her place clearer. All I'd have to do would be solidify the threat. Put the fear of the devil in her.

Then do intermittent check-ins to make sure she's still scared.

Intimidation is an easy game, really.

But that's not tonight's show.

I don't know what the fuck I'm going to do with her, but everything in me rebels at the thought of scaring her even more than I have. And honestly? She's a tough cookie because so far, the only thing that broke her was the closet and the risk of not making her deposit.

So she trusts me against her better judgment, or she trusts herself to be able to handle me.

I don't mind either of those scenarios.

We pass a motor cop giving tickets out. Hannah's head jerks up.

I tense, a million ugly scenarios running through my head, the primary one involves her trying to open her door and jump out. But she immediately looks over at me. Nothing surreptitious about it. Not hiding what she just saw. More like she's questioning me—did *I* see that cop?

I cock a brow. I really don't understand this girl.

"What happens if you get pulled over?"

My brain scrambles to follow. Is she for real?

"You worried about me?"

She shrugs. "You don't have a license."

I throw on the brakes when I see someone pulling out and put on my blinker behind them. While we wait, I give her a total stare-down, trying to get into her head. "You scared of me at all, Flowers?"

I should want her answer to be yes. It would mean I've done what needs to be done to keep her quiet. Ensure she doesn't talk. But for whatever dumbass reason, I love that she's not all that scared. Because she's into me.

Her eyes widen slightly like I just reminded her that she should be. "Yeah." She sounds breathless.

"Not enough to want me busted."

She's still holding her breath when she gives her head a little shake.

Huh. Not sure what I did to win her allegiance, but I like it.

I park and throw my door open, walking around swiftly in case she runs.

She doesn't. She hops out and tugs down her short skirt, which rides tight over those shapely thighs. Her mess of curls falls over one eye as she contemplates me.

I hold out my hand like we're on a date and she invited me in instead of whatever the hell I'm doing with her.

"I've had enough of hand-holding with you." She flounces past me without taking it.

Something foreign and buoyant stirs within me. Something I haven't felt in years. What is it?

Amusement.

The girl amuses me.

That's my lips trying to curve, but they don't remember how.

I ignore the urge and follow her.

Chapter Twelve

annah

H We walk up the stairs to my apartment, and I try to remember if I cleaned out Shadow's kitty litter this morning. My place is tiny, and it can easily start to stink.

But that's stupid—am I really worried about what he thinks?

It's not like he's some guy I invited to come up to Netflix and chill. He's a mobster who killed a guy in my shop today. He's taken me, my van and my apartment hostage, and I have absolutely no clue how this thing ends.

The only thing that keeps me from totally freaking out is his obvious attraction to me. Even now, walking up the stairs, I sense his gaze on my ass.

I turn around to verify. Yep.

"Like what you see?" I say dryly.

"Oh, Flowers," he says. "I am *all about* your ass."

I turn away before he can see the satisfaction on my face. This guy hasn't been with a woman in years, and I'm his first lay, so, of course, he's going to think I'm all that.

Even so, his lusty reaction to my kiss back at the shop forever changed me. I don't ever want to be with a guy who gives me less of a response.

It's not that I don't usually get attention. I do. I get plenty of it. Men all over my thing. But it never lasts because I'm the idiot who always gets attached too quickly. I'm an emotional sponge, and I get into their worlds. I feel their emotions for them. Try to fix their problems. Forget about my own. And then suddenly, I'm all in, and they're walking away. Like clockwork.

Seriously, I've dated too many man-babies. Immature players who are more interested in themselves than anything else.

Armando is...

He's extremely capable. And very dangerous, yes. I'm sure in some twisted way that's part of the attraction.

And I remember once upon a time, he used to be charming.

Now he's damaged.

He's been in prison, just killed a guy in front of me and then tied me up and fucked me immediately after. He's probably very damaged.

I'm crazy to be so turned on by him. What is it about the bad boy that makes a woman think she can reform him? It's a losing proposition, I'm sure. He may be sexier and more capable than the usual guys I date, but my pattern of wanting to fix is the same.

Some secret instinct in me wants to heal him.

I think that's what made me give myself over to him. Made me kiss him. Offer my body up to quench his desperate need.

I wait for him at the door because Armando has my purse. He fishes out my keys and hands them to me. When my fingers shake trying to slide the right one in the lock, he takes over, opening the door and ushering me in with a hand at my back.

My apartment is just a studio and a bathroom. Fortunately, it doesn't smell.

The front door is painted the color of a bumblebee, something my landlord would shit over if he knew I painted it. But I needed color in all the drab.

Inside, my apartment is simple and small. The one room is furnished with a small two-man purple sofa, a coffee table with a colorful tapestry flung over it, and a TV I bought at a thrift store for thirty bucks. The kitchenette has four cabinets and a small refrigerator. I'm lucky enough that this unit also has a two-burner stove unlike some of my neighbors. There is barely enough room for a tiny table and two chairs, but I was able to cram them into the space.

My bed is up against the far wall in order to give me as much room as possible. I have colors of the rainbow splattered in pillows across a bright blue comforter to make it appear as a lounge area rather than what it is—a bed crammed in a small room with a sofa.

Twinkle lights are strung from one side of the room to the other, casting a warm hue on the space. It might not be much to most, but it's mine, and I feel comfortable inside.

The kitten mews from the bed, standing up and arching his back in a shivery stretch. "Hi Shadow." He runs to me on tiny paws and twines around my ankles.

I watch Armando as he moves around my space, unsure of how to read his expression.

Eyes usually give away the feelings that hide behind people's masks, but when I look into Armando's eyes, all I see is a void. His entire being seems to have built a wall between us that I can't penetrate. A sensation of unease and unfamiliarity crawls up my spine as I try to connect with him.

Still, there is something oddly comforting about his presence that makes me feel safe. Ironic considering...

"So what happens now?" I demand, pretending I'm not scared of the hulking man beside me.

Armando rubs his face. "Now?"

I'm pretty sure he doesn't know. There's no script for the I-killed-a-guy-in-your-florist-shop scenario.

"Now I'm going to sit on you until I'm sure you're cool."

"I'm cool," I assure him immediately. I guess I've been waiting for him to ask me. Or demand it or... whatever. I've already decided—if I hadn't from the very beginning—that I'm not going to rat on him. "I'm not going to tell anyone what I saw. I won't say a word, I promise."

He nods. "Good."

"So... we're cool. Right?"

"Not yet."

I huff out a sigh. "So what are you going to do?"

He leans his back against the door and scans my apartment. When his gaze dances over the bed in the corner, his lids droop, but he gives his head a shake and pulls out his phone. "First I gotta make a call. Then I'll order us some food. What do you like?"

I shrug. Don't mind a free meal, considering there's nothing but a couple cans of flavored seltzer water and a bag of potato chips in my kitchen. "Anything."

He arcs a brow. "You eat calzones? I know a great place."

"Sounds good. I'll have whatever you're having."

He dials a number, and I hear a short, clipped conversation. Mostly *yeah* and *thanks*. I head to the bathroom. While I'm there, I hear him order two calzones, a salad, and a bottle of wine, rattling off my address, which apparently, he's already memorized.

I use the opportunity in the bathroom to quickly clean out the kitty litter although why I'm working so hard is beyond me.

This is not a date.

I hustle out of the bathroom with the tied trash bag of cat poop and run smack into Armando's big chest.

He catches my wrists then wrinkles his nose and pushes the one with the trash bag away from our bodies. "Do you want it to be a date?"

What?

Oh crap, did I mutter that out loud? I thought he was on the phone!

I pull out of his grasp, practically dashing for the door.

He catches me around the waist right before I get there. "Where are you going?"

I hold the bag up. "To the dumpster. I'm not leaving this in here." I use my best *duh* voice.

He doesn't release me. Instead, he holds me even tighter, his mouth coming to the outer shell of my ear. "Keep up the sass, Flowers. I'd love to spank that ass again."

My knees buckle.

Dammit. That was not swoon worthy, but for some reason, my body thought it was. My pussy clenched when he said it, and now all I feel is a hot, slow pulse. The throbbing complaint of that missed orgasm. Maybe one more time with him, just to finish, just to feel if all this heat lives up to its hype would be worth it.

"*You* take it then." I know—I sass. It's not even subconscious.

Luckily—or maybe unluckily—I'm not certain, he

doesn't take the bait. Instead, he slowly releases me. "Can't do that, either."

"Looks like we're going to have that date, after all. I always wanted a guy to take me to the dumpster." I toss my hair as I look over my shoulder at him.

He lets me go, and when I turn, I glimpse an echo of the old Armando. His lips quirk like he might smile if I keep it up. He takes the knotted trash bag from my hand and interlaces his fingers with mine. "Nothing's too good for my girl."

I hide a grin as he opens the door and hooks his index finger through the loop on my keys as we leave.

Shadow darts out, and I stoop and pick him up and rub my face in his fur and kiss his sweet head before I drop him back inside and shut the door.

I want to keep up the flirting, but an awkward silence descends between us. At least, it's awkward for me. Armando's as tense as ever. Same hard blank face he wore cleaning up a dead guy. Driving my van.

We walk down the three flights of stairs and outside to the dumpsters then back again without saying a word to each other. Armando glances around outside, doing his badass secret agent impression again.

I wonder who he's worried about.

"So who's trying to kill you?"

Nothing changes on Armando's face. He doesn't look at me. But I see a muscle flex in his jaw like he's grinding his teeth.

He ignores my question and quickens the pace back into the building.

I think through the facts. He just got out of prison, and someone's trying to kill him. So it's either something unresolved from when he went in. Or maybe something that happened on the inside.

"You kill someone first?"

His gaze cuts to me then away.

So that's it. Someone wants revenge.

"Is it someone from within the mafia?"

"Seriously, Hannah." His tone is all business. "Ask another question, and I'll tape your mouth. I mean it."

I'm more offended by the threat than I should be. We're both pretending I'm not his prisoner. I guess I prefer that fantasy to the terror that goes with the harsher picture of what's happening here. Or how this might end.

"You're a dick," I mutter.

Nice comeback.

"I'm trying to protect you." Does he sound slightly defensive?

I scoff. "Yeah, you're a real knight in shining armor, aren't you?"

His own scoff is soft and bitter. "Definitely not that. And you don't want to know all the depraved things I'd like to do to you, so don't tempt me."

Now I do want to know.

About the depraved things.

I want to know so badly... I might ask him. We bump shoulders as we climb the stairs side by side.

"What depraved things?" Apparently, I have no self-control.

He gives me that heavy-lidded look that makes my panties damp. He makes a sound in his throat and then says, "I might tie you to that bed."

And? I desperately want him to go on.

Chapter Thirteen

Hannah

My nipples are tight beads. My pussy's wet and slick. I'm hungry for a re-do, so I can come. I also realize how insane this is. Me, seducing my captor. Or was he seducing me?

What in the hell are we doing?

We step inside my apartment, and he closes the door behind us.

"I'd spread your legs wide and lick that pussy until you screamed." His voice is rough and raw.

I remember again how much passion he brought to our hookup back at the shop. How he's fresh out of prison, and I'm the first woman he's been with.

"W-what do I have to do"—I swallow—"to get that treatment?"

Armando grabs me by the hair and claims my mouth as he walks me backward until my knees hit the bed. I fall back onto it, and he follows, climbing over me, lips twisting over mine.

I would've said the kiss we shared back at my shop was

the best of my life, but this one might be even better. It doesn't carry as much desperation, but now I get some finesse. Like a violent kiss followed by a quick nip. A trail of kisses that run down the side of my throat.

"Now you're in trouble," he murmurs as he pins my wrists above my head. "Big trouble."

I writhe beneath him, lust blasting through me. I swear I've never had this kind of reaction to a guy before. I've been excited, especially if I've had a drink or two, but the way my body reacts to Armando now is off the charts.

Our first hook up was a lightning strike. This time, he goes slow. He bites through the layers of my crop top and the camisole beneath it to scrape his teeth over my nipple. My legs wrap around his waist, pulling him in tighter. I twist my hips, trying to find satisfaction rubbing against him. He reaches down and pulls something out of his pocket. I think it's going to be a condom, but it's the roll of floral tape.

Like he *planned* on tying me up again.

And that thought should scare me way more than it does. But with the way his mouth is on mine, I can only interpret his actions one way: the tape is for sexy times.

He winds it around my wrists—not nearly so tightly as he did back at the shop—and pushes my wrists back over my head. He leans up on one hand, gazing down at me. His pupils are blown, eyes full of dark intent, but his face is expressionless. Like he's forgotten how to smile.

He traces his thumb lightly down the inside of my arm. I squirm when it covers the most ticklish part.

"You didn't answer me before."

He sounds so gruff. So serious. If it weren't for the light touch, I would think he was pissed.

"About what?"

"What part turned you on—being tied up or spanked? Or the other thing?"

The other thing. I guess that's him grappling with a guy in a fight to the death.

It definitely shouldn't have turned me on. Except I always had a thing for those Jason Bourne movies, and Armando looked every inch as badass as Matt Damon. Or Chris Hemsworth in that Netflix movie *Extraction*. So yeah, up until the actual death part, it tweaked the most primitive part of my brain. The part that seeks to reproduce with the fiercest warrior in the land.

"All of it," I murmur.

He stares a moment longer, without saying anything. Like he's trying to read into the depths of my soul. Then he asks, "You like it rough?"

My face grows warm. I'd be a fool to admit such a thing with a guy I can't trust. Besides, I don't know if it's true. Before today, I hadn't tried it.

"I liked it rough with you." That's the truth—and all I know, really.

Something shutters behind his eyes, and he reaches for my wrists, pulling my arms long over my head and attaching them to the bedpost.

Shivers of excitement run through me at my helplessness. The thrill of being completely at his mercy focalizes every sensation to a sharp point. He shoves my two shirts up and tugs down the front of my bra roughly. I gasp a little, my belly shuddering in and out with my breath, my nipples bead up into stiff peaks. He pinches my right nipple between his thumb and forefinger and squeezes. Hard. Then he slaps the side of my breast.

I croak in surprise. I'm scared—definitely scared—because it hurt a little, and no one's ever touched me that way before. There's a disrespect to it, too, that I'm not sure I like.

Except he watches my face intently.

And that steady regard calms me.

He pinches my nipple again then drops his head to suck it. He laves it with his tongue, scrapes his teeth lightly over the taut bud, pulls it into his mouth and releases it with a pop.

My lips part. Brain fries and scrambles.

He gives the treatment to the left nipple, only he starts with his mouth and ends with a slap.

I cry out, startled once more. I'm a little frightened, a lot turned on. He pinches both nipples at the same time, rolling them between his fingers and thumbs and pinching before he expands his grip to encompass all of the breast.

I drop my head back and arch, filling his hands with my breasts, begging for more.

Armando moves lower, his large palms sliding up my skirt, skating lightly up my thighs to my hips, then hooking under the waistband of my panties and dragging them down.

"I didn't make you come enough before, did I?" His voice is a rusty rumble. "You're a greedy, greedy girl."

I shake my head.

"I'm gonna make it up to you this time."

My breath comes out in a low moan.

He tosses the panties to the side and runs the pad of his thumb over my dewy slit. "Juicy," he observes.

I'd be embarrassed, except he brings his thumb to his mouth and sucks my fluid like it's honey. "Spread."

I stare for a moment, taken aback by the command. He grips behind my knees and pushes them up toward my chest, then slaps the inside of my thigh. It smarts, and I don't like it, but then I forget because he lowers his head between my legs.

The first lick makes my hips jump off the bed. He slides his hands under them and grips my ass, squeezing and releasing as he strokes his tongue up and down my slit.

Crazy sounds come out of my mouth. Strangled sobs. Little *uhn*s. Choked breathing.

I moan and arch and thrash my legs around his shoulders.

He takes his time. The tip of his tongue traces all around my inner lips, then flicks over my clit. He uses it to penetrate me, then puts his lips over my nubbin and sucks.

I scream, yanking on my bound hands, my knees crashing around his ears. He sinks his thumb into my entrance without releasing the suction on my clit, and I start to shake and shudder. I'm close—so close—to release. I just need him to pump that thumb in and out, and I'll get there.

Only he doesn't.

He slides his thumb out. Breaks the seal on the suction.

"No-o," I moan. "Please."

"You want to come?" His voice is so rough and deep I scarcely recognize it.

"Yes. Please. Do it again, Armando. Oh God, please?"

"You gonna be a good girl?"

"Yes!" I don't have any clue what he's talking about, but I will definitely be a good girl. I would do anything he wanted me to at this point.

"If I say *spread*, what do you do?" He brings his fingers down in a light slap over my clit, and my knees snap closed and flap open like wild butterfly wings.

"Spread. Oh God, I'll spread. I'm sorry—I was slow before."

He sinks his thumb into my entrance again, and I moan

with satisfaction. I can tell how swollen and wet I've gotten. How much I need this.

"Please," I plead again.

I've never begged for it before. Never needed it like this.

If he would just pump that thumb, I'd be there. Or suck my clit again. I flap my knee-wings some more, trying to take his thumb deeper.

I'm shocked by the sensation of a finger at my anus, and I tighten against it, whining.

"Nuh uh." He shakes his head. "Open for it."

Oh God. Really?

I don't want it. Except I do. Because as that digit works against my back hole, my temperature rises at least eight degrees, and I start moaning like a porn star. It's taboo and wrong, but it feels so good.

He pumps, alternating between his thumb and other finger, then pumping them both at the same time. The moment he leans over and rides my clit with his tongue, I come—*hard.*

So incredibly hard.

Like so hard fireworks dance before my eyes, and I close my mouth around a full-on scream.

The room spins. Lights continue to flash and pop behind my lids. My pussy and anus squeeze around his digits, and I sob out every last bit of pleasure I have in me.

I don't know how long it lasts. I get lost somewhere on another plane.

I open my eyes when he starts easing out, and it feels like I've been gone forever.

Armando's expression is inscrutable as usual.

And that's when the doorbell rings.

Chapter Fourteen

*A*rmando

I'm hungry, and the timing worked out the way I'd planned, but I'm still pissed to have to answer the door.

I reach up and break the tape holding her wrists and pull her up to sitting, tugging her shirt back down over her rumpled bra. I don't want the delivery guy to see her like this.

I don't want the delivery guy to see her, period.

I'm feeling extremely fucking possessive of her right now. I help her to stand and steer her toward the bathroom. "You go get cleaned up. I'll get the door," I give her ass a slap.

I swear to Christ, that ass was made for slapping. I could seriously punctuate every sentence with a slap to that ass and never get tired of it.

She scoots off to the bathroom, and something shifts in my chest.

Her surrender does something to me. She's not weak or stupid or even scared. At least not too scared. I think she's genuinely submissive. It explains her sexual response to getting tied up and handled. I haven't experienced a woman like her before. Her trust feels like a gift. One that makes me feel strong and weak at once. Humbled.

Highly protective.

I wait until the bathroom door is closed before I open the front door and pay the delivery guy. I drop the food on the tiny two-person table by the window and look for plates and wine glasses. Her place is tiny, but it's cute. She has plants in colorful pots everywhere. Some are flowering, some are wrapped in bright bows. Her furnishings are rustic —white washed shit. Probably flea market finds, but it has the look of purposeful design. Rich people pay a lot of money for this kind of look. She's definitely artistic. She has a real eye for this stuff.

I was going to put the calzones on plates and open the wine, but the sound of the shower running makes my dick throb. My balls are so fucking blue from licking her pussy, I can barely walk.

I should leave her alone. Let her shower.

Instead, I find myself testing the bathroom door. And when I find it open, I take it as an invitation. My clothes drop to her floor before the thought to strip even forms. I pull back the shower curtain and step in.

Her eyes widen, but she doesn't recoil. She stares at my body. I look down. I've been so damn disconnected from it, I don't even know what I look like anymore. My chest is hairy, and I lack any color from the sun. I was bigger when I went into prison. The extra layer of meat has hardened into sinew and muscle.

She doesn't seem to mind what she sees because her lips part like she wants to taste me. I take my time running my gaze all over her luscious form.

It's perfect. She's short but curvy, with a narrow waist, round breasts and heart-shaped ass. A chain of flowers is tattooed around her upper arm with a small, winged fairy sitting on the top of one of the buds. Her skin is a smooth brown. She's nothing like the kind of girls I've been with before. She's real. Beautiful.

I watch the rivulets of water stream over her dark nipples. I want to lick the droplets from them. Scratch that. I'm *going to* lick the droplets from her skin. I pull the curtain closed behind me and pin her against the tile wall, my mouth moving over hers with all the force of pent-up aggression.

I don't know if it's going nearly five years without sex or because Hannah does something special to me, but I can't seem to dial back my sexual aggression with her. Fortunately, she's willing. Her arms loop around my shoulders, and she lifts one leg around my waist to give me the angle I need to get inside her.

"Condom," she gasps between kisses.

Condom. Fuck. How could I forget it?

"Don't fucking move," I growl, pinning her back against the wall with my hand between her tits and waiting a beat for my order to set in.

Then I yank back the shower curtain and fish in my pants pocket for a condom out of my wallet. I rip it open and stand, rolling it over my length.

"Good girl," I say because she hasn't moved an inch from where I left her. "Come here." I pick up her thigh and find her entrance with the sheathed head of my cock, prodding it until I find the sweet spot where it starts to slide in. "That's right," I murmur as I feed the head in slowly. "Take it."

She grips my shoulders, pulling me closer.

"Take every inch." I keep pushing forward, all the way, until I'm fully seated. Then I prop one foot on the tub, her thigh draped over the top of mine, and start thrusting.

It's pure heaven. The last time I fucked her, I was out of my mind with need. This time, I savor every sweet thrust. The slick of our skin sliding together, the heat of her tight welcoming channel.

I take her hands from my shoulders and pin them up against the tile. Not for me—I like the feel of her nails scoring my skin—but for her. Because I'm testing what she likes. How she likes it. It works—maybe too well because her eyes roll back, foot slips. I hold her wrists with one hand and use the other to hoist her ass up, holding her in place.

I should say something—praise her. Tell her how much I like it. I used to know how to dirty talk up one side of a building and down the other. Now I'm so fucking rusty at speaking to another human being. I force my lips to move. "So good, Hannah." It comes out like gravel. Or sandpaper. Deep and ragged. "You feel so good."

She moans softly, and I take it as encouragement.

I don't want it to end, but my hips have a mind of their own, snapping hard, pumping deeper.

She starts making those sexy noises again, and my brain short-circuits. I get too hot from the warm water and steam and my blood pumping straight to my cock. My head's getting light, which isn't good, since I'm the one holding us up.

I pull the shower curtain open by a foot to let in some air and fuck her harder. I forget to hold her wrists because my hands are roaming her body, squeezing her breast, gripping her waist, kneading her ass.

"God, you feel so fucking good," I moan, my voice breathy and hoarse. She arches her back, pressing her chest against my own, and I swear I feel her heart beating in rhythm with mine.

I'm lost in the sensation of our slick skin sliding against each other and the warmth and pressure from her tight grip around me. I'm so close... just a few more thrusts, and I'll go over the edge.

But before I do, I reach one hand around and slip my fingers between us, finding her clit and circling it softly. She gasps, and I feel her walls quiver around me as she comes.

I brush my lips against her neck, sending trails of tingling sensation down her spine as I continue to thrust into her.

My breathing gets faster as I feel my climax approaching, and I grab onto her hips tightly as I plunge deeper and deeper into her, wanting to savor every moment. She cries out as her body convulses around mine.

My balls draw up and pump. I shout and grip her ass with both hands and then bury myself deep as I come. She tips her pelvis to take me deeper, rubbing her clit over my root until she comes, too. Her muscles squeeze my dick in quick pulses, and I come even harder, filling the condom.

I lean my forehead against hers, breathing with her, my dick pulsing and twitching inside her. Our mingled breaths slow. The water's turning cold. I don't want to ever pull out, but I do. I ease out and turn off the water, then step out of the shower to dispose of the condom. The water ran all over the floor because I opened the curtain, so I drop the hand towel down on it and wrap Hannah in the other one. She's still leaning up against the tile looking dazed, so I help her out of the tub, supporting her in case her legs don't work.

She points shakily at the cabinet, murmuring something unintelligible. I open it and find another towel, which I use to dry off.

"Wow," she murmurs.

I turn to face her as I towel off my hair. "Yeah. Thanks."

"So... Are you going to let me go now? Are we cool?"

I go still. Blink. The room swoops around me. I drop the towel on the floor. What the fuck is she saying?

A rushing sound starts up in my ears.

Did I just... *rape a girl?*

Did she think she had to do that for me to set her free?

"Is that what this was?" I choke, not even realizing I'm advancing on her. Not conscious of my hand caging her throat and pushing her back. "Is that why...is that...*fuck!*" I roar and punch the wall beside her. The plaster caves, and my knuckles go through it.

"Fuck." I release her and turn away.

Did she just offer herself up to me in hopes I'll set her free? What kind of monster am I?

I can't even tell when a girl wants me or not. I've gotten so confused, stuck in the modes of violence and survival, I don't even know what's real.

I thought I could manage this situation with Hannah. Had some vague idea about how to keep her from getting hurt by me or the organization, and instead I did the most unforgivable thing.

I pick up my clothes from the floor and pull them on, my chest cracking open as Hannah opens the bathroom door and makes her escape from me.

I follow only because the steam in the bathroom's making me dizzy, and I really fucking need to think.

I hear a stifled sob, and bombs explode in my chest, down my arms, in my gut. Hannah's got her back to me at her dresser, trying to get her second foot in a pair of panties and missing. I should give her space. I definitely shouldn't go to her.

But I do.

In a second, I have an arm banded around her waist to support her wobble, and I reach down to hold the waistband of the panties for her. I slide them up when she gets her leg in and just hold her from behind.

"I'm sorry," I murmur against her hair.

Her chest shudders on a sob. She stands still for a moment, like she's listening. "Sorry for what?" There's a quietness to the question.

It's some kind of test, but I don't know what it means. Like there's some answer I need to give that will make this all better. All I fucking know is the sound of her stuttered breath kills me.

Because all emotional intelligence I once had—if I ever had any—is long gone, I mutter, "Whatever made you cry."

It's the wrong answer. I know as soon as I say it. I know it even better when she squirms away from me, whirls and slaps my face. It's a wimpy slap and half-misses me. It clearly didn't give her the satisfaction she was going for because she curls her fingers into a fist and throws a punch instead.

I dodge it, catch her wrist and wrap her arm in front of her waist. With my other arm, I scoop under her knees and lift her into a baby-carry.

She gasps and struggles. "What are you doing?"

I don't know what I'm doing—why I picked her up or what I'm going to do with her now. All I know is that I don't like the chaos in my chest. In my head.

I carry her to the bed and set her on it, yanking the sheet off the corners to cover her bare breasts. I sit beside her on the bed. I want to hold her, but my touch is obviously not welcome. "I just—" I try to unravel what just happened. She's more pissed now than she has been throughout this whole thing. Which must mean it was something I said... I review what just transpired between us and... *ah*.

I'm an idiot. I asked if she had sex with me, so I'd let her go.

She glares at me, lower lip trembling with obvious offense.

"Hang on, Hannah. Let's straighten this out. I wasn't calling you a whore. I didn't mean any disrespect. Not at all. I was—" I draw a breath, trying to find words to explain the rage inside me. "I was pissed at myself."

The rage settles. Like identifying its source was what it needed.

"Did you feel like you...had to? With me? I didn't—did I force you?"

"No, asshole." She shoves my chest.

I welcome the touch. It's still a connection—something I've lacked for ages. And she didn't try to punch me this time. I catch her hand and hold it there. "Talk to me." I'm practically begging. The words are rusty in my mouth, but I keep pushing them out. "I'm so outta touch with this shit, Hannah."

I watch a tear track down her smooth, flawless brown skin. "I'm trying to stay on this ride with you and not freak out, but...." She takes a shuddering breath and holds it then releases it slowly. "You can't touch me when you're angry like that."

White horror blankets through me. *Cristo*, did I hurt her? I reach out to tip her chin back, examining her neck for bruising, but I see nothing—no fingerprints, no marks. I swear I didn't hurt her—I wouldn't. Not even out of my mind as I was. It's just not in me to hurt a woman. "I didn't hurt you—did I, Hannah?"

She shakes her head.

"I scared you," I guess. Of course, I fucking scared her. I held her by the throat and broke the wall beside her head.

"No." She pushes my hand off her neck and looks away. "It's not that." Her voice is tight. Frustrated.

I am so fucking lost here.

"I don't know if I can explain. Just don't do that again."

My heart beats faster like my body knows this conversation is gonna be important if I can just figure out what the hell we're talking about. "Try me. Try to explain."

She turns her gold-flecked brown eyes back on me, considering. "I'm one of those people who..." Her eyelids flutter down like she's embarrassed. "I don't know—it's like I sense everybody else's emotions. In my body." She gestures with her hand up and down the center of her trunk.

I cock my head. "An empath." Like from *Star Trek*. Is it a real thing?

Apparently.

The flicker of hope that sparks in her expression tells me I finally said something right. "Yeah, I guess. If someone in the room cries, I cry. If someone's upset, I get upset. So just... don't touch me when you're mad. It's too much for me."

Shit.

I finally get it. I channeled the shame and anger I felt straight into her body. Or she experienced it that way.

"Fuck." I reach for her, and she doesn't flinch away. I pull her closer to me and lift her onto my lap, adjusting the sheet to keep her covered. "Okay, Flowers. I won't touch you when I'm mad. Swear to Christ."

She tucks her face against my neck. After a moment, her lips move, kissing me softly.

I can't explain what happens in my body. It's like all my organs sort of lift a half-inch. Like I've been in a pressure cooker, and it pushed everything down. And now my insides regained form.

I resist the urge to tighten my arms around her. The need to stand up and shake off all these foreign emotions is too strong. "Let's eat," I say gruffly, lifting her from my lap to her feet and squeezing her ass.

Chapter Fifteen

Hannah

I pull on a camisole and pajama shorts. Dang it. I *hate* when I cry in front of people. It's so damn embarrassing. Me and my overblown emotions. This is how I scared off every guy I've ever dated.

Armando seems to move past it quickly, though, which is a relief. He unwraps the calzones and drops them onto plates then pours red wine into my juice glasses.

"Sorry, I don't have wine glasses." I slide into the wicker chair I found at a flea market and painted a cheery yellow.

Armando's gaze drops from my face to my braless chest and lingers there as he settles into a chair that matches mine in paint color only.

My nipples bead up at his attention. I swear it's like I've just been mega-dosed with breeding hormones because no matter how many times we do it, I seem to want more.

"It doesn't look like you have a lot of things," he says. "What were you going to eat for dinner if I wasn't here? Your refrigerator doesn't have any food."

I shrug. "I'd figure something out."

Armando scowls. "You should be taking better care of yourself."

I roll my eyes. His protectiveness is sweet, but I'm a grown woman, and I'm not sure I like the idea of being lectured.

"I am taking care of myself," I say. "Just because I don't have a fancy refrigerator stocked with all the latest and greatest doesn't mean I'm not taking care of myself." I smirk. "But thanks, *Daddy*, for caring."

"Maybe that's exactly what you need. A daddy to take care of that ass of yours." He slides closer, his dark eyes full of promise.

My breath catches in my throat. I should push him away and tell him that I'm not interested. But I can't. I want him, even though I know it's dangerous. I take a deep breath, trying to steady my pounding heart, and whisper, "Maybe I do." I flutter my eyelashes. I'm trying to play this game of seduction but I'm probably failing.

"A daddy to spank you when you've been bad," he continues.

My face heats as my eyes meet his. I want to look away, but his gaze holds me. I'm rooted in place, mesmerized.

"I think you'd like that, wouldn't you?"

I open my mouth to protest, but I'm too flustered to respond. I just shrug, not trusting my voice. I don't want to give away just how much he's turning me on—again.

Heat rushes to my cheeks. Armando smirks, his gaze dropping to my lips then back to my eyes. His intense stare says that he's not just being playful. He's serious.

"Do you want a daddy? Do you want a man to take you in hand and tell you what to do?" His voice low and husky.

I swallow hard and shake my head. "Please. Like you could." My fake resistance is obvious, I'm sure, but no way can I admit just how much that question sent shivers down my spine.

Armando moves closer and reaches out to stroke my hair. His touch sends electricity through me, and I close my eyes, savoring the sensation. "Maybe I need to change your mind."

"Good luck trying." I wonder if my feelings are written all over my face. "Besides, you're just a guy who semi-kidnapped me. I mean, is this a kidnapping or a date? Can we have some clarity here?"

He gives me one of those unfathomable looks and takes a huge bite of his calzone and chews. "Kidnapping with benefits?"

I hide a smile with my own bite. "Oh God. This is so good." A long line of cheese trails out of my mouth, and I go out wide to break it.

"Right? Missed the fuck out of Gio's."

I study him. He's coarse-mannered but gentlemanly all at once. A tough guy, for sure, built of taut deadly muscle but no tattoos. That surprised me. "Are you staying the night?"

He gives a single nod. "Definitely."

"What happens tomorrow?" I'm halfway through the calzone already. I didn't realize how hungry I was until now. That granola bar I had for lunch was a long time ago.

Armando wolfs his food down too. "I'm still sitting on you. Until I'm sure."

"What would make you sure?" I press.

He shakes his head. "Stop. Just stop."

I wait, thinking he's going to say something more, but he doesn't. He just takes a swig of wine.

"Fuck this." I stand and wrap up my remaining calzone. If I eat any more, I'll get a stomachache. "You're getting the benefits. I'm the one who's kidnapped. I think you owe me a little more information."

He doesn't move, but his gaze on me is intent. "You're benefiting too." It's not a question, but I sense that he's asking again. He's careful about this. It's what upset him in the bathroom, when he thought I was trading sex for my freedom.

I have to appreciate this code he's operating under. He'll kidnap me, but he won't harm me. I know because of the way he freaked out when he thought he gave me the cat scratches. He'll dominate, but he won't coerce me into sex.

Weariness suddenly sets in. Maybe it's the wine or just the intense stress of the day, but I suddenly want to fall down on the floor in a heap. Or cry some more.

I turn away from him, blinking back sudden tears.

Screw this. I'm going to bed. I head to the bathroom to brush my teeth.

I hear him washing the wine glasses. Putting things away.

I remake the bed, which he screwed up when he pulled the sheet out to cover me. Another gentlemanly gesture.

Stop making lemonade out of lemons. I am the definition of Stockholm Syndrome right now.

I climb in and pull the covers up to my waist. "Can I have my phone back? If someone called or texted, they're going to think it's weird if I don't answer."

Armando scrubs a hand across his face. "I'll check it."

I'm deflated, not because I need my phone but because I'm not getting anywhere with him trusting me. I watch him retrieve my purse from one of the cabinets—I guess he hid it from me there—and pull out my phone. He looks at it. "What's your passcode?"

I hold out my hand for it, but he doesn't move. Damn

him. I'm going to lose any battle of wills here—I'm way too flexible a person. "Five-five-five-five."

"Lucky fives, huh?" He punches it in and looks at the screen. "No messages."

His phone rings. He pulls it out of his back pocket and looks at the screen. "Hey."

He listens. "Tonight? Fuck." His shoulders sag, and he looks across the apartment at me. "I'm trying to lay low." He listens some more. "Yeah, I gotcha. No, no, I'll do it. I'll be there. In an hour. 'Kay." He ends the call and shoves the phone back in his pocket, then he gives me a long, appraising look.

The hairs stand up on my arms. "What?"

He marches over to my dresser and starts pulling open drawers.

"What are you doing? What do you need? Just *tell* me, asshole."

He looks over at me and shakes his head. "Don't call me names, Flowers." He opens my sock drawer and pulls out a pair of tights.

"What are you doing?" Alarms are going off like crazy, but stupid me, I'm still playing like this guy's my date. Later I will wonder why I didn't fight him. Didn't run.

He crosses swiftly to the side of the bed and picks up my wrists and starts wrapping the tights around them. "I have to go out. I can't take you with me."

"What? No!" Even now, I don't fight much. I'm still relying on my ability to persuade him to change his mind. The guy has a conscience, I know that much.

He knots the tights and wraps the end around the bedpost.

"No! You can't leave me here like this. What if there's a fire? I will die because I can't get out. *Armando!*"

He ignores me and goes back to the kitchen area rummaging through the drawers. When he returns with a roll of duct tape I really freak out.

I kick out at him in a panic, yanking at my wrists to get free. "No! You're not putting that on me!"

Shadow, picking up the energy, races around the room and then under the bed.

Armando rips off a piece. I turn my face away.

"Don't!" I shout. "I am never having sex with you again. I swear to God."

"I understand." He slaps the tape over my mouth. I scream against the constraint. I have to take crazy snorting breaths through my nose because I'm crying.

"Shhh." He caresses the side of my head.

I yank away.

He crouches beside the bed face level with me. I'm hyperventilating through my nose. "Take it easy, Flowers. I'll be back as soon as I can."

I shake my head frantically.

"I'm sorry. The other options would be worse, I promise."

Tears flood my eyes. I'm so pissed, I want to headbutt him. Too bad he's out of reach.

"I'm gonna take your van, so I can get back quickly. Just go to sleep. I'll be here when you wake up."

I scream in my throat and shake my head, but he catches the side of my face, plants a quick kiss on the tape over my mouth and straightens.

Dammit. I missed the chance to headbutt him!

Asshole.

And then he's gone. And I'm tied to my own bed with a pair of tights.

Chapter Sixteen

A rmando

Marco says Don G is out at his strip club Lollipops, so I'd better get my ass over there and report.

The fact that you just whacked a guy is not the kind of thing you say over the phone, and Don G wouldn't want me coming to his house with that shit, either. We don't talk business around the women in the family. We leave them and all the innocent out of it. It's part of the code.

It makes me sick that Hannah didn't get left out of the pile of shit I'm in because tarnishing her might become the thing I regret most.

And here I thought I'd lost my conscience altogether.

I drive her van to Lollipops but park it a few blocks away. I don't want anyone making a connection between me and my little florist. Someone's still trying to kill me, and I can't have her caught in the crossfire any more than she's already been.

I stalk into Lollipops, and the whole gang is there. It's the old crew—Don G's inner circle, minus Alex, his son-in-law. He'd already been like a son to Don G, and he ended up marrying his daughter while I was in the pen, so I'm guessing he's permanently banned from Lollipops out of respect to Jenna.

Funny, at this moment, I wouldn't mind the same. The girls twirling around their poles do nothing for me. Neither does the male company.

Lollipops is a reputed strip club in the city. It has an old-school vibe to it, with neon signs on the walls and velvet-covered furniture. There are two stages at the back of the room, each with its own pole, where two dancers will perform simultaneously. Two large bar sections fill the main area of the club and a few smaller tables littered around for more intimate conversations. The music blasts from speakers set up around the club and seems to fill every corner of the room with booming bass.

The walls are adorned with black and white photographs of former dancers as well as signed photos from other celebrities who have visited over time. While there is a decent selection of drinks available, it is mainly focused on beer, wine, and whisky since those are mostly what people come here for; there aren't many cocktails or mixed drinks on offer.

The girls who work here wear costumes that range from barely skimpier than lingerie to some quite daring outfits—often leaving very little to imagination when they take center stage on one of the poles to show off their skills. They move gracefully around their poles in time with the music, quickly shifting between different dance moves such as pirouettes, splits and twerks while they seductively gyrate their hips or flick their hair around like silky ribbons in mesmerizing displays which usually draws loud cheers from their audiences.

At either end of both stages stand two large LED screens displaying clips from movies—usually action flicks —that serve as background distraction for those not captivated by what is happening onstage at any given moment. Occasionally special performances are put on where the dancers will use props and interact with the crowd— usually met with a lot of enthusiasm from everyone in attendance.

Overall, Lollipops has an air of old-school glamour infused with sin and debauchery.

But I sure as fuck don't want to be here. Especially because I keep seeing Hannah's teary face and picturing her trapped in flames. *I will die because I can't get out.*

I know the chances of her apartment building going up in flames are slim, but dammit, now I can't stop thinking about it.

I should have called someone to watch over her while I was taking care of business. Have someone sit outside her door. What the fuck was I thinking leaving her alone? I know better than that. I protect what is mi—

"Hey, there he is! Mando, come over here." Angel beckons me over. I shoot a glance at Don Pachino chewing his cigar, but he's got a guy on each side vying for his attention. I'll have to wait my turn.

"Everybody buys Mando a lap dance tonight," Angel announces. "Make up for lost time."

Lost time.

There was never a better descriptor for my years in prison. Not the way he means, like I lost out on part of my life—which is accurate. But for me, the time is also semi-lost. I shut down in the pen. I mean, physically I was still alive. I slept and ate and walked around. I fought for my life. Killed a man with my bare hands. But I don't remember anything.

Correction—I don't *want* to remember any of it. So it's definitely lost time.

"Nah, I'm good. I just came to have a word with—"

"Bullshit." Angel pulls me down into the chair beside him, already signaling one of the dancers with a twenty between his fingers. "Give my friend here a dance, sweetheart. He just got out of prison."

I definitely don't want the dance, but I do what I'm supposed to do—slump down in my chair with my arms loose by my sides and my thighs wide, making myself a jungle gym for the girl to rub her cheap fruity perfume all over.

"Don't say that again," I tell Angel. I know I'm an asshole. It's disrespectful as hell. He's from the older generation and a capo, and the organization is all about respecting our elders. I sense him bristle, so I add "Please."

"Yeah, all right." There's a grudging tone to his voice, but he's going to let my bad behavior slide, since I'm fresh out. I got this one free pass. "I get it."

He doesn't say sorry—of course, I don't expect him to—but we're *simpatico*.

The dancer does her thing, pushing her breasts in my face, straddling me, then turning around and grinding her bikini-clad ass against my dick.

She's wearing a tiny red thong and eight-inch stiletto heels that she uses to keep me in place. Her back is arched, her head thrown back, her long blonde hair cascading down across her shoulders. She gyrates against me like a slow-motion wave, and between the sheer desperation of her act and the fact that I'm stone cold sober and not even trying to hide my discomfort—it feels like I'm stuck in some awful time warp. She looks over at me every few seconds with sad eyes as if begging for mercy, but all I can do is just sit there motionless, waiting for it to be over.

I work to wait for the shit to be over. I seriously don't have the patience for this tonight.

It's hard to imagine I ever will again. Did I really used to enjoy nights like this down at the don's club? Playing the big man. Working hard to fit in, to play the role.

Now I just want to walk away.

From it all.

But that's not an option. You don't get out of *La Cosa Nostra*. Not when you're a Made man. Don Pachino owns me now, for the rest of my life.

Arturo waves another girl over with a bill. "Your turn. On him." He points at me.

Fucking Christ on a clamshell. How long will I have to endure this?

But I know if I don't, everyone's gonna read it the wrong way especially the Don. I gotta show my gratitude, be good natured here. Yeah, I did time, but it's part of the game. Now I'm out, and they treat me to lap dances and help me set up my life again. I gotta prove I'm worth the effort they're putting in. Also, that I haven't rolled over or gone sour.

That's always the fear when someone's fresh out of the pen. Especially when they're out a year early. But I know better than that. That's a line I would never cross. Not outta fear, either. I *am* still loyal. This *is* still my family.

I'm just not feeling it right now.

But I'm not feeling much of anything, so that's not unusual.

Fucking Emilio sends over another girl, and instead of waiting her turn, they give me two-on-one, a girl's tongue in each ear, their hands all over my fucking clothes.

My cock is semi-hard because, yeah. Tits in my face. But I'm more low-level disgusted by them than I am turned on.

And honestly? If I'd come here last night—before Hannah—I don't know if I would've even sprouted a chub. Hannah woke my dick from the dead.

And—fuck—she's tied up and gagged right now in her own bed. That's the way I repay her.

I am never having sex with you again. I swear to God.

I deserve that. But I'm also asshole enough to hope she'll get over it. Because right now, she's my fucking lifeline. She's the only thing that even seems to make sense—and considering how fucked up our interactions have been up to this point—that's saying something.

"I got your next one," Marco calls out to me.

"No, I got it," Leo offers.

I shake my head and Marco nods, grinning like there's nothing going on. "All right. Next time, then."

The dances finish, and I stand up before anyone else can send over a girl. Fuck this. I know I'm being rude. I should stay a few hours, drink a few drinks. Prove my loyalty and work my way back into the inner circle.

But that's not happening. I walk over to Don Pachino and stand in front of him, giving Emilio the death glare until he says, "What?"

Of course, the guy's too much of a prick to take a hint. "I need to talk to the don," I say.

"Give him your seat," Don G mutters, and only then does Emilio get up, purposely bumping my chest as he passes by.

Johnny, the guy on Don Pachino's other side, also gets up, presumably to give us privacy.

"What's wrong?" Don G says immediately.

I sink a little lower in my chair, keeping my gaze trained on the dancing girls on the stage. "Someone has a hit out on me. A cleaner showed up this afternoon outside Rocco's. I took care of him. Just thought you should know."

"Who sent him—someone from prison?"

"Yeah. Probably. I iced a gang member on the inside. Might be revenge for that. I don't know. I'm staying low until I figure shit out. I won't let it affect the job you gave me or any Family shit. *Lo prometo*."

"Call in sick to that job for a few days. You get paid time off. Let things settle. Figure this shit out."

I nod my head and stretch out my hand to shake the don's. "All right. Will do. Thank you, Don Pachino."

"Don G," he corrects, clasping my hand and letting me know I'm still inner circle. Only his closest soldiers called him by the more informal moniker Don G, for his given name, Giovanni.

I stand and nod at the rest of the group.

"Hey, Mando, want another dance?" Arturo calls.

"Not tonight. Thank you. 'Preciate it. All of you." Jesus fuck. I have to force the niceties over my dry lips, and they all sink like ashen lies.

I can't play this game anymore.

I remember I used to be so good at it. The best. Now it's like I'm playing a stranger's part. It all feels so foreign and wrong.

I beeline it out of there and to Hannah's van.

Fuck—*Hannah*.

I sure as hell hope she fell asleep.

Chapter Seventeen

Hannah

I jerk awake when I hear Armando come in, and Shadow, who was curled up in front of my chest, jumps off the bed and stretches. I blink at the digital bedside clock. It's been two hours since he left. I slept fitfully for the last hour after I finally calmed myself down with slow breathing. Now all the adrenaline of the stressful day rushes back, so I'm wide awake. And still very pissed.

He comes straight to my side and crouches in front of me. "You're awake." He peels the duct tape off my mouth.

"You're an asshole."

He ignores that and unties my bound wrists from the bedpost. The moment they're free, I swing them at his face. His reflexes are way faster than mine. He snaps them up in an iron grip. "Hey." He modulates the grip, loosening slightly. "You want to spend the night tied up?"

"Go to hell."

He stops work on the knot on my tights and arches a stern brow. It's tragically sexy, which pisses me off even more. I shouldn't find any of this hot. He's confused me with sex, blurring lines, so I can't tell what's what. Actually, I guess I'm the one who started it with that kiss back at the shop. But now, I'm a jumbled mess. It's like I just willingly dove headfirst into an abusive relationship where I'm bonded to my abuser, craving his affection and ignoring the fact that he's holding me prisoner.

It's way worse than all the misguided relationships I've been in. Worse than Jarod, who cheated on me three times before I stopped believing he was sorry. Worse than Eric, the guy it took me six months to realize only thought of me as his booty-call. This is the definition of a toxic relationship. It's not even a relationship. It's Stockholm Syndrome.

Ragey tears fill my eyes again, and I fight some more, wrestling to get my bound hands free.

He tightens his grip, dropping a knee on the bed to hover over me, pushing my hands closer to my chest to trap me. "Hannah."

"You stink of cigar smoke," I hurl at him, like he's a lover come home late from a night of partying with the boys. Then I catch another cloying scent on top of it, and my stomach drops out. "Oh my God! You're covered in shitty perfume! You fucking dick!" I'm unprepared for the flood of betrayal that fills my lungs.

"Hey, hey, hey, hey." He straddles me. Somehow, he worked the knot loose on the tights while I flail at him, and he pins my wrists down beside my head. One wrist is still wrapped in the fabric. I keep fighting him, the pain of my stupidity for screwing this guy gushing like blood between us. "I was at a *strip club*," he says like that makes it all better. When my mouth elongates in horror, he adds quickly, "For a *meeting*."

Right. Apparently when you're in the mob, that's where

meetings take place. On second thought, I'm inclined to believe that part.

"Everyone bought me dances because I'm fresh out. I wasn't into it, Flowers."

"Oh, I'm sure you weren't." My voice drips with hurt and sarcasm.

His face contorts into scorn. He normally shows so little in his expression that it takes me aback. "You think I needed that shit? After what you gave me?"

I go still.

After what you gave me.

Armando's face hovers inches from me, his hazel eyes sparking. There's frustration in him. Passion. I feel it through his skin, but it doesn't harm my body this time—it feeds it.

"If you fucked another woman tonight, I'd cut off your dick." I may be his prisoner at the moment, but I'm still going to make myself clear. I'm not stupid enough to believe our sex today meant anything—I didn't take it as a promise or a commitment. It just happened. But I would take huge offense to him dipping his wick elsewhere after what we did.

"I didn't, Hannah. I didn't even want to be there. I swear to Christ." He suddenly looks so weary. His eyes, ancient. "And you had me worrying about a fucking fire the whole time."

Well.

That's sort of satisfying, too.

I'm still pissed but growing mollified.

He pulls the wrist with the tights still wound around it to the bedpost and starts retying it.

Fresh alarm rings through me. "What are you doing?"

"Rinsing the smell off." He pulls my other wrist up and secures it, too.

For me, a little voice whispers.

"You are such an asshole."

He's back to cool and indifferent, his face the brutal mask. "Been told that." He heads to the bathroom and leaves the door open while he strips out of his clothes.

I watch. He's not putting on a show for me. He probably left the door open to make sure I don't scream or try anything, but it's a show worth watching, nonetheless. I saw him naked earlier, but that was up close, and I was half out of my mind with lust. Now, I can observe him clinically. And he's even more impressive the second time. He's solid muscle. Six-pack abs, the kind you could climb. He's not shiny. Not tanned and waxed and all-American. He's hairy, brutal, and strong. He's grit and manliness.

My dad is a kind, working-class man whom I deeply respect and love. He's a big, strong guy who can fix anything with his hands. He works in construction as an electrician. Union guy.

Even though Armando is more of the slick Italian suit type, there's something about him that resonates for me. Some similarity between them that hits me on a biological level. My brain imprinted my father as the archetypal man. Armando fits the archetype. He's strong. Take charge. He gets shit done.

Armando steps into the shower. He's quick about it, soaping everywhere and rinsing off in no more than two minutes.

He pulls on his boxer briefs after he dries off and returns to the side of the bed. He doesn't speak as he unwinds my tights from the bedpost. He doesn't untie my wrists, though.

Maybe he thinks I'll try to punch him again.

I still might.

He climbs in the bed beside me. I keep my back to him, my shoulders hunched. I'm still nursing my piss-off.

When he molds his body to mine and wraps an arm around my waist, I swing my bound arms back to elbow him. He's too fast. He catches my wrists and ties the loose end of the tights to his own wrist. Ah. Now I understand. He wasn't trying to spoon me. He's attaching himself to me.

I imagine he considers it to be kinder than keeping me tied to the bedpost. I guess it is. This position's better, anyway.

And I secretly enjoy the feel of his arm draped over me, the weight of it. It's centering. Comforting in ways it shouldn't be. It's been a long time since I've been held by a man, and I forgot how much I love it. The scent of soap and clean skin enters my nostrils.

His cock twitches against my ass.

"We're not having sex again," I say firmly. Maybe I'm trying to convince myself.

"Understood," he rumbles.

"I mean, ever."

"Shh, Flowers. Go to sleep." He wraps his big hand over the top of my bound ones, almost like we're holding hands.

Because I hate how much I like it, I say, "I still think you're an asshole."

He doesn't answer, and I start feeling guilty, like I should worry about hurting his feelings.

Then he speaks. "Listen, I know you're pissed, Hannah. But trust me, tying you up and leaving you here was the best option I had."

I turn my head in his direction, staring angrily at the ceiling. "That is such bullshit."

"Would you rather I left you tied in the van in the strip club parking lot? Or—fuck. I'm not even going to tell you the other possibilities." Frustration laces his words.

A shiver runs up my spine because I suspect they involve getting rid of me—the only witness to his crime —permanently.

And I'm suddenly as weary as he looks. Maybe I'm just soaking in his state, but it's a crushing weight. Tears pool in the corners of my eyes, and one slides down my nose. "What about the option where you just trust me? I told you I won't talk. When will you believe that?"

Armando is silent behind me, but his body is stiff and tense. His arm has tightened around me and so has his grip on my hands. Finally he exhales loudly into my hair. "I do trust you, Hannah. It's just that the stakes are too high here to go on trust. If I make a mistake, it will cost me my life."

Okay, those *are* high stakes.

"I'm sorry you got caught in the crossfire. I really am. But shit went down that I didn't plan, and now I'm just trying to manage the mess."

"And I'm part of that mess."

"You're the only good part," he says. I think I feel his lips brushing the back of my neck, and I try to stifle the shiver of pleasure that runs through me. Try to steel myself against his words, even though I believe him. I know they're true.

"Don't leave me tied up again." Tears clog my voice.

He pulls my body back against his snugly. "I'm sorry, Flowers."

Earlier I was sure sleeping with my wrists bound would be impossible, but I already find myself sinking into a deep relaxation, the heat and weight of Armando's body like one of those weighted blankets that are supposed to be so soothing.

"I don't want to hurt you, Hannah," he rasps into the darkness.

He already has. But I think he knows that.

I'm an emotional sponge, and that makes me soak in all his feelings.

So I believe him. I have compassion for his situation. But it doesn't mean we're not speeding toward a brick wall. Or that it won't hurt like hell when we crash.

Chapter Eighteen

*A*rmando

I jerk awake several times during the night, my heart pounding, the instinct to kill sharp as a knife edge, but each time, when I find my body wrapped around Hannah's soft, warm form, my pulse slows. Each time, I bury my face in her hair—her incredible curtain of tight curls—and breathe in her scent, and I'm home.

Being near Hannah is like opening a trap door and discovering a whole different world exists on the other side. She's not wild, not crazy, but she functions in a way that's so outside of the norm—so far from what I've known—that it's slowly waking me up from the stupor I've been in.

All the emotions, all the passion and flexibility and kindness. Soft strength. Every minute with her changes me. I'm coming back to life.

Except it's not my old life. Not a life I've known before.

It's something so different and bizarre, I don't even know how to think about it.

I untie our wrists and free her hands while she sleeps,

tracing a fingertip over the vines tattooed on her shoulder and down her arm. She's so fucking beautiful. So unlike any woman I've dated before. The polar opposite of Grace. Her beauty is so natural. The wild mane of hair that falls to her ass, her short, curvy but muscular body. The tiny gold nose ring. Her smooth brown skin. She's unpretentious and down-to-Earth.

I sift her wild mane of hair, letting the golden-tipped curls wrap around my fingers.

I want to trust her. I do.

But I can't be stupid and reckless. I can't think with my dick.

Still, I've treated her like shit, and for the most part, she's taken it. I need to do something nice.

I pull out my phone and go online shopping. It's a stupid gift. Definitely not something she needs, considering she doesn't even have food in the refrigerator or a van she can rely on. But then, aren't the best kinds of gifts the ones you wouldn't buy for yourself? I enter the Garden of Eden address for delivery and complete the transaction.

Sleeping beauty still hasn't woken up.

Hunger finally gets me out of bed, but when I get up to rummage, I find nothing in her kitchen. I'd leave to go get something, but I don't want to tie her up again. And I don't want to wake her, either.

I find a nearby cafe connected to one of those food delivery companies and order an egg sandwich and latte for each of us.

And then I start looking through her shit.

I open her drawers and look inside. Check out the art on the walls, which mostly consists of photographs or paintings of flowers.

I don't know what I'm looking for—clues about who she

is, I guess. Nah, that's a fucking lie. I'm looking for signs of a boyfriend.

I know she doesn't have one, or she wouldn't have fucked me, but I want to know if she dates. Who she's dated. What her history is.

Did she fuck other guys the way we fucked?

Or was that special?

Because it sure as hell wasn't normal for me.

Course, I've never gone five years without sex before.

But I think our connection is more than that. Our chemistry is off the charts. The way she gives herself over to me brings out the fucking dominant in me, which I didn't even know was a thing.

I mean, yeah, I like to lead. I'm an alpha male and need to be the guy in charge. But I was always respectful. I didn't bend women over, smack their asses and get nasty with them. I never tied a girl up before.

Course, that wasn't for fun, it was a necessity.

The first time.

And the last.

But not the time in between. That time, we both liked it.

Hannah brings out the fucking savage in me. It's crazy the things I want to do to her. Even now, when I'm thinking about buying her shit, I want to semi-force myself on her again.

Not real force. Not in a way that pisses her off. But play force. Or half-force. Like at the flower shop when she was scared but turned on. That's how I want her every time.

Trembly. Nervous. Surrendered.

Of course, right now, sex is off the table. She's pissed at me, and I won't push it. I owe her my respect.

Hannah wakes up when the delivery guy rings the

buzzer. I'm rooting through her underwear drawer, checking out all her panties.

"What the hell, Armando? Are you perving on my panties?"

Definitely, *amore*. I drop the pink lacy pair I'm holding back into the drawer. My cock's pressed up against my zipper from me picturing her in those panties, picturing pulling them off her—with my teeth.

I don't answer as I buzz the delivery guy up.

Hannah wraps her arms around herself like she's scared. Or feeling vulnerable. "Who's coming?"

"Just food, Flowers. You hungry?"

Some of the tension drops away from her posture. "Yeah." She doesn't leave the bed, though, so I just open the door a crack to accept the food then bring it over to her. She eyes me warily as I hand her the coffee and set mine down on the nightstand.

I completely lost her trust last night. It's probably better this way. She should be scared of me.

I climb on the bed and sit with my back against the wall beside her while she takes a tentative sip of the coffee and then moans softly.

"It's good?" I ask.

"So good. What is it?"

"Just a latte." I look at her curiously.

"It's stronger than I usually get. Or, less sweet. I usually get the kind with all the sugar and syrups and stuff. I didn't think I'd like it this way."

She's talking to me like everything's normal. It eases some of the chaos in my chest that's been there since I made her cry last night.

I open the paper bag of food and hand her the wrapped

breakfast sandwich then take out mine. Her kitten, Shadow, jumps onto the bed and pads over, purring. I eat my sandwich, careful not to let any crumbs fall onto the bed and ignore the little thing, but he chooses my lap to curl up in, his little paws playing the piano on my thighs.

I finish eating and push the wrapper back into the paper bag. The kitten stands up to investigate, putting his little nose in the bag then reaching a paw in to touch the crinkly paper.

He's still purring.

I open the mouth of the bag and change the angle, so he can get in, and he crouches down and slips inside, turning around and making the bag bump and move as he does.

Hannah makes a small sound of amusement beside me.

It's cute. I *know* it is, but I don't quite feel it. It's like the centers in my brain where all that shit takes place got turned off. I picked up that kitten last night when we first got here. Looked right in its face, knowing intellectually it was cute as hell, *trying* to feel something, but I hadn't. Same as how I didn't feel anything when I hugged my mom at that welcome home party. And a mom-hug is usually the thing that brings on all the emotions, even if they're mostly shame and regret.

But Hannah's tears did something to me last night. She makes me feel.

That's something.

She's still eating, her bites delicate, and her chewing slow. I climb out of bed and pick up my coffee, carrying it to the bathroom where I search for a razor and shave my face.

When I come out, Hannah's getting dressed. She's wearing a grey t-shirt dress that hugs her every curve, with a white lace midriff top layered over it. She has on an artsy pair of chunky sandals in turquoise, tan and orange. Her toes peek out, toenails painted hot pink with tiny white flowers. I want to suck on those toes.

She turns to face me, her face taut. She's nervous.

Fuck. Is she afraid of me now? I should be glad, but it's like getting kicked in the gut.

"I have to go to the shop." There's a challenge in her words, but a slight twitch in her lips belies her bravado. "I have flowers to sell, and if I don't sell them, I can't pay the bills." She lifts her chin, her nostrils flaring slightly as she pins me with her demanding gaze.

"What time?" I ask mildly. I'd kinda figured she had to work. I'd seen the hours posted in her window.

She blinks a moment, like she's surprised I didn't say no. "I open at noon."

I glance at the clock. It's already ten. "You ready?"

Her body springs to life, and she takes a quick step toward the bathroom then stops. "Um… what's happening, Armando?"

"I'm staying on you, Hannah—until I'm sure. So we're both going to the shop."

"This is crazy." She mutters and pushes past me to enter the bathroom, but the tension's gone out of her. Like before, it seems she's more worried about her business than she is about me. And for some reason, that lightens my mood, too.

I pull her purse out of the cupboard where I stowed it and grab her charger from the desk. I put her phone in my back pocket.

She comes out of the bathroom with makeup on and a colorful piece of fabric wrapped around her head, keeping her curls out of her face. She's wearing mascara, and her lips have a sheer color on them. I want to kiss it off, but I know better than to try.

"Let's go." There's another challenge in her posture.

I hand her the purse and take the keys.

"This is so weird," she says when I lock her door behind us. "I am trying to roll with this situation, but if I think about it too hard, I'm pretty sure I will flip out," she says as we walk down the stairs.

I put my hand lightly on her back. I shouldn't touch her —not after last night—but her body's irresistible. I want to have my hands all over her, all the time. "I'm amazed you haven't, Flowers." I rub my forehead. "You've shot straight to the top of my list." I stop myself because I don't even know what the fuck I'm saying. Only that it's true. She is way at the top of my list. Of everything.

"What list?" she asks. Because, yeah, that was a weird thing to say.

I shake my head. "Nothing. Nevermind."

She slides me a sidelong glance, curiosity brewing under those thick, curled lashes.

It hits me then: she likes me. That's why she kissed me. It's the reason she hasn't freaked out about me marauding her life. Invading her space. I mean, I knew there was mutual attraction. Off-the-charts chemistry. But I see something else now. It's the good old-fashioned girl-likes-boy current running from her to me. A desire that's more than sexual.

And fuck if it doesn't make me almost want to laugh.

Not *at* her. Definitely not. No, it just lifts so much weight off my chest, I could soar.

I thread my fingers through hers. She may be pissed at me, but she still likes me. I'll earn back the right to touch her.

When she doesn't shake me off, I revel in the small

victory. I walk her to the van and open the passenger side door for her.

The van sputters, taking four times to start. Fuck. This needs to get fixed. Today.

Chapter Nineteen

annah

H I definitely didn't expect Armando to let me go to work. I thought we were going to have another throw-down that I would lose. And I also didn't guess he would come with me.

It's weird and wrong that I'm semi-excited by the idea. Like my boyfriend is coming to hang out at work with me.

I keep reminding myself I'm his prisoner not his date, but then he holds my hand and opens my door, which sends my body into a riot of flutters and thrills.

I wasn't totally paying attention to the route he took, but when he turns into a car repair shop, I sit up straighter.

"What are we doing?"

"Getting a new alternator in this thing. Come on."

I grab my purse, open the door and hop out, noting he's not snarling orders at me not to move any more. Trust is growing.

"I don't have money for an alternator," I tell him when I walk around. I figure he already knows, but it's best to be clear.

"I got you covered," he says.

"I can't let you do that," I say.

His face morphs to one of an authoritarian. "I'm not asking. I'm telling you that the van isn't safe or reliable. So, I'm fixing it. This isn't open for discussion."

It shouldn't be swoon-worthy, but there's something about the way he says it that makes my nipples go hard. It's a flash of the old Armando—the slick, smooth-talking guy who used to come into the shop when Mary Alice owned it and flash huge wads of cash. It's that confidence and ease, a bit of swagger. Like money is no problem, and he's happy to provide. Definitely sexy to me.

He talks to a mechanic, telling him what he thinks is wrong with the van, and then we step inside to fill out paperwork. He has them fill it out in my name but gives his phone number and name as the contact then asks for a shuttle ride to the shop.

It's not that hard, but I've been overwhelmed by the idea of even bringing the van anywhere since the problems started. Mostly because I knew I couldn't afford any repairs. But also because I was afraid they'd take one look at me—a young Black woman who knows nothing about cars—and try to screw me over.

Nobody would ever try to screw Armando over. At least not anyone in his right mind.

He's silent on the ride to the shop, sitting beside me but actually somewhere far away.

I nudge his leg with mine. "Thanks."

He turns his head and looks at me, no hint of a smile, his face that dangerous, blank mask. I don't think he even heard me. "What?"

"I said thanks."

He blinks at me for a moment more, like it takes a while

to come back to the present and process my words. Then his gaze drops back away. "My pleasure, Flowers," he mutters.

I think about slipping my hand into his, but I resist. I can't even imagine what he's going through—fresh out of prison with someone trying to kill him. He committed murder and took the witness as his prisoner. A squeeze of his hand isn't going to fix this.

I'm lucky my problems are fixable, and he's willing to help me solve them. If he hadn't bailed me out with the rent yesterday, I don't know what I would've done. And getting the van fixed will be huge for my goals of getting the business profitable. Starting deliveries again.

The shuttle drops us off at the shop, and Armando unlocks the door, looking left and right down the street, secret agent style. His gaze travels over and lands on the place where the body fell.

"Are you all right?" I touch his elbow.

Armando jerks and turns, lifting his brows. A puff of air escapes his lips in a *tuh*. "You're asking *me*?" He settles his palm at the back of my head and brings his mouth down to my temple. "Are you?" His voice is deep and quiet. There's an intense intimacy to the question, like we share a deep secret, which I guess we do. He smells clean, his freshly-shaven skin is smooth against mine.

My heart picks up speed. I become conscious of how close his lips are to my skin. How comfortable his grasp on me is. "Yeah, I'm okay. I didn't know the guy, and it was... sort of unreal to me. Like watching a movie, you know?"

Armando nods. Behind my head, his thumb massages my skull. "Yeah. Same for me. But my whole fucking life feels like I'm watching a movie right now. Everything except—" He stops.

I pull back to look at him. "Except what?"

His fingers slide in the back of my hair and tighten into a fist, capturing a section of hair. He uses it to tip my head back. "Except for you. You feel real to me."

I stop breathing.

He moves slowly, like he's giving me time to protest, and lowers his mouth. He slides his lips over mine. It's an elegant kiss. An experienced one. Not like that mad, hot claiming when we kissed yesterday.

This is different. This is seduction.

And seduction is definitely not playing fair. Because Armando isn't the kind of guy I can fall for. This isn't love. I may have played dirty when I first kissed him, but he's definitely the one playing dirty now.

I manage to get my hands between us, and I push on his chest at the same moment I pull away. He allows it, rubbing his lips together like he's savoring the taste of me.

I stumble backward then turn and hurry into the back, turning on lights and getting things ready to open shop.

Crap. I need some distance from this guy. Because, right now, he's so up in my world, he's in every pore. Which makes it very hard to put up any lasting defenses.

My hands shake as I move around the shop, my mind and body still overwhelmed by his kiss. I can't deny the heat that still lingers between us, and I know it won't go away anytime soon.

I try to focus on work, but my thoughts drift back to Armando and the way his lips felt against mine. A deep warmth spreads through me as I remember the electricity that passed between us.

I pause and look up, only to find him standing in the doorway, watching me with a smoldering look. I hold his gaze, and for a moment, neither of us move. Then, he steps closer and reaches out, running a finger along my cheek. His touch is gentle but firm, sending a wave of pleasure through my body.

His eyes scan me up and down, and my skin heats up under his gaze. "You're so beautiful," he murmurs, leaning in to whisper against my ear.

I shiver, my heart racing as I try to find my voice.

"You're trying to distract me," I say. "From work."

"Is it working?"

"I open soon, and I'm not ready." Jesus Christ the man is dangerous. The power he has over my body is undeniable.

Armando takes a step closer. "You look ready to me."

"Armando..." I begin, but I'm cut off by his lips pressing against mine. This kiss is different from the first, more intense and passionate. And I can feel the tension between us rising with every passing moment.

Finally, he pulls away and looks at me with a heavy-lidded gaze.

"I understand if you don't want this." His voice low and husky. "But I can't deny what I'm feeling right now."

I nod, my heart pounding in my chest. I want this, too. But I'm scared. Scared of what will happen if I let him in.

"I... I want this," I whisper, my voice barely audible.

He pushes me in front of a tall shelf that I use to store ribbons and decorative items for my arrangements. Pinning me against it, trapping me between the hard surface and his body. His hands move up my sides, and I can't help but arch my back, pushing my body closer to his. He leans forward and presses his lips against mine, his tongue slipping inside my mouth, exploring and tasting me.

My breathing becomes shallow, and all I can feel is his hard cock promising me of what's to come. His hands slide down my back and cup my ass, lifting me up and pressing our bodies together even more. I wrap my legs around his waist, and he reaches down and effortlessly rips my panties off.

Armando kneels down before me and begins to kiss my inner thighs, slowly working his way up until he finds my clit. His expert tongue caresses it, and pleasure spreads through my body. He moves his tongue up and down, teasing me until I'm panting with desire. His hands slide around to my ass, and he pulls me closer, thrusting his tongue deep inside me. I moan in pleasure, my body trembling. I arch my back, pushing myself closer to him, urging him to go even deeper.

He responds by slipping a finger inside me, his thumb finding and rubbing my tight bud. His thrusts become more urgent, and I can feel myself reaching the point of no return.

My moans grow louder, and my body is shaking as I reach my climax. His hands slide up my sides, and he slowly stands to meet my eyes again.

"Ready for more?" His voice is low and husky.

I nod, my body still trembling from the pleasure he just gave me. He kisses me deeply and turns me around, pushing me against the shelf once more. I hear the sound of a condom wrapper being torn open—or at least I hope that is what I hear, but I'm too far gone to care.

"You said you would never have sex with me again." His husky words caress my flesh and send a shiver down my spine.

"I changed my mind," I somehow reply.

He drags the head of his cock over my slit, then enters me from behind, filling me up with each thrust, and I let out a loud moan.

He moves faster and faster, and soon I'm screaming out his name, grateful I haven't opened for business yet.

His hard thrusts become more and more intense, and I sense another orgasm building up inside me. As I reach my peak, I feel his body tense, and he releases a deep moan as he thrusts. He pushes even deeper, and I can feel his warm cum filling me up as he finally reaches his own climax.

We stay like that for a few moments, panting and trying to catch our breath. He pulls out of me and wraps his arms around my waist, resting his head on my shoulder.

Signs of my completion coat my inner thigh, and I glance to my panties cast to the floor.

He spins me around and kisses me deeply, his hands lingering on my body. His touch is electric, and my arousal quickly rises again in response. He moves his lips from my mouth and trails down my neck, sending shivers over my skin.

He slides his hand lower and presses two fingers inside me, circling them around until I'm quivering with pleasure.

"I like feeling your juices. I like how they coat my finger," he says.

I moan in response, desire and need coursing through me. He continues to flick and tease, his thumb now brushing against my sensitive bud and sending waves of pleasure through me. I arch my back and push against his hand, wanting more.

He moves his other hand to my hips and holds me firmly in place as he caresses my core still trembling from my climax. My legs tremble beneath me, and I'm left gasping for air as he slowly withdraws his hand.

He wraps his arms around me again and whispers in my ear, "I owe you a new pair of panties."

Chapter Twenty

*A*rmando

I sit in the workshop area to stay out of Hannah's way. On one wall is a long workbench with shelves above it that have all her materials like vases and baskets and the green foam things that you stick the stems of flowers in. This is where she puts together her designs. On the narrow half-wall is her desk, covered in stacks of invoices and old school ledger books dating back thirty years. Mary Alice's shit.

Hannah moves quickly through the place, arranging things in the cooler, tidying up. Then she turns the open sign around and props the door open.

I start sifting through the invoices and paperwork, making a quick mental tally of the totals as I go. She's done three weddings in the last three months—those pay big. But the rest of the stuff is all small- time bouquets and arrangements. Looks like deliveries stopped four months ago. That must've been when the van started acting up.

For kicks, I pull down the most recent ledger and open it. I used my time in prison to get a degree in business. I guess I was thinking I'd impress the don when I came out. I haven't even told him about it yet.

Despite my lack of enthusiasm for much of anything right now, business still interests me. I open the ledger and look through the receipts and payments. Arturo had me use an old-fashioned ledger like this to record our car heist income and payouts, so I'm familiar with the layout. I pull out the next ledger and the next. The entries I see reflect the strain Hannah's under. Mary Alice's income hadn't grown in years. It had only maintained. And her profit margin hadn't been huge to begin with. The major expenses were employees and rent. The flowers and other materials are next.

Hannah walks back and jerks to a stop. "What are you doing?"

I don't answer—instead I ask, "You paying the same expenses Mary Alice paid?"

She steps closer, her body rigid. "More or less. The rent went up by two hundred when I took over, and I also have to make monthly payments to Mary Alice for the business."

"How much?"

"Fifteen hundred."

I give a low whistle.

"What?" There's a mountain of defensiveness in her voice.

I shouldn't push, but I want to dig into this. Figure out what went wrong. "You run the numbers first before you entered that deal?"

She goes a little pale. "What do you mean?" When she pushes her hair over her shoulder, I see her hand shaking. She may be perfectly capable of handling me—a legit killer who's taken her prisoner—but she's over her head when it comes to running her business, and she knows it.

I catch her trembling fingers and hold them. "Ah, I just mean, I can see why you're hurting. There wasn't much wiggle room to begin with."

She stares down at our joined hands like they're foreign objects. Christ, she looks like she's going to pass out. She pulls out of my grasp to hold onto the edge of the desk and blinks rapidly.

"Hey—don't freak out. It's workable. It just means you can't do the same thing Mary Alice did and expect to make any money. You gotta make changes."

She leans heavily on the desk, like her legs aren't holding her up. I want to pull her into my lap and tell her everything's gonna be okay, but I'm not her hero. And I'm too cynical to believe it's gonna work out unless she changes strategy.

"What changes?"

I stand up and fold my arms across my chest. "I don't know. You gotta drum up new business. Make new connections. Work new angles. You're paying Mary Alice for her good will—the steady business she had—but you might be overpaying. And that business has dwindled."

Hannah's eyes fill with tears, but she blinks them back. Someone walks in, and she hurries out to the shop floor, throwing a death glare at me over her shoulder when she arrives.

I keep an eye on her. She's within earshot, so I could hear if she asked the customer to help her and see if she tried to slip them a note or something. Honestly, I don't expect her to try anything, but I'd be stupid to blindly trust. No one does that, especially not when it comes to a beautiful woman.

Hannah rings up a cheap bouquet for the woman, sending me another angry glance over her shoulder.

I crack my neck. Why do I feel like such a dick?

I was only honest, and I was trying to help.

Still, I don't like seeing her pissed. Same as last night—when I left her tied up—something uncomfortable slithers in my gut.

Feelings.

Fuck.

Do I even *want* to feel again?

Maybe life is fucking easier when you're numb and can't make yourself give a shit about anything.

I should stay and keep a close eye on Hannah, but I'm itchy to solve my own shit and end this fucked-up situation with her, so I pull out my phone and walk to the back of the shop to call Luis, a guy I used to know. He owns a pawnshop and is happy to move things off the books, too. He's a fence of all things big and small. He's connected with most everything underground in Chicago—including the gangs.

He picks up with a "Hey."

"Hey, it's Armando, from the Pachino Family. Been a while."

"Armando. You out?"

"Yeah, just got out."

"Whatcha got for me?"

"Nah, nothing. I'm staying legit, but I wondered if you could help me with some information."

He pauses. I know nothing in this world comes free. There will be a price for anything I get from Luis. "What info?"

"There's a hit on me. Wondered if you'd heard about it?"

"Nah, I don't know anything about that. Who do you think it is?"

"I'm guessing the Hermanos. I had a run-in with one of

their members on the inside. Could you find out if I'm right?"

"Yeah, I'll ask around. This your new number?"

"For the time being."

"'Kay. Be in touch."

I hang up and open the back door to the alley, feeling restless. Something got me thinking this morning that it might not be the Hermanos at all. Seems like they'd do a drive-by with a bunch of guys and automatic weapons. That was more their style. Sending a single guy to plug me on the corner screams hired hit. And why would they hire a hit when they're all perfectly capable of killing me themselves?

Only two reasons you hire a hit: you aren't a killer yourself, or you don't want it known you're responsible. And when I say don't want it known, I don't mean proven. I'm not talking about cops knowing. I mean known on the street.

Say Don Pachino puts a hit out on someone. He's sending a message. He wants everyone on the street to know he's responsible for it. I would think the same goes for the Hermanos. The message would be *don't fuck with our guys in prison or on the outside.*

So a hired mercenary coming after me seems strange.

I don't like it. And it gets me thinking maybe I have more to worry about than I thought.

And now I'm getting fucking paranoid.

Like thinking I shouldn't have ordered from Gio's last night. People know me there. The owner would know my name. And I used a debit card, which means now they have me connected to Hannah's address. So I might've ruined my plan of laying low at her place.

It's the reason I took her van to a random mechanic this morning. I know mechanics. Guys who would give me a great deal on it or even do the work for free. But there is no way I'm gonna link Hannah and her business to my name. She's already in this shit deep enough. If something happened to her because of me, I wouldn't be able to live with myself.

I watch her at her workbench, putting together new arrangements. She's talented. And in over her head.

I want to help her.

It's the first thing I've been clear on—apart from wanting to fuck her—since I got out. First thing that's generated even a spark of interest.

Too bad me getting involved with her business is the worst idea. If I really did care about her business, I'd stay way the hell away.

Chapter Twenty-One

annah

H My stomach is in a knot up under my ribs. Or maybe that's my diaphragm on lock-down. Must be because I can't really breathe. My stress level shot to freak-out mode when Armando was asking me about the business.

Tears prick my eyes as I make up bouquets I don't need. Working with the flowers is the only thing that makes me happy here, though. I mean, it makes me happy in general—that's why I gave up my scholarship to nursing school—my mom's plan for me—to buy the flower shop. Flowers make me happy. I like their colors, their delicate textures, their smells. I love that I get to work with such a beautiful medium and use my eye and creativity in the arrangements.

College didn't suit me. I may have been a straight-A student, but that didn't mean I enjoyed it. No, when Mary Alice approached me to take over, I wanted this more than anything in the world.

But now it seems like I made a huge mistake.

Armando walks in from the back door, and I frown at

him. There's a little bit of hate rattling around in me toward him right now.

I know it's not his fault, but he told me the thing I've been hiding from myself for the last six months. I made a huge mistake buying Garden of Eden. I gave up my education and sure-thing career, and now I am going to lose everything.

"Hey." He leans a hip against the bench and watches me. "I wasn't trying to piss you off."

"I'm not pissed," I lie in a tight voice. What I really mean is I don't want to be pissed because it isn't his fault I'm drowning here.

"I wasn't criticizing your decision or your business, Hannah."

Sure as hell isn't how it feels.

"Look at me."

I ignore his command.

"Hannah." He plays Mr. Forceful very well. I'll bet he makes guys pee their pants when he wants to.

I turn to him with lips tight. Pressure bottlenecks in my throat, threatening to explode.

"You're not totally fucked. And you didn't fuck up, either."

I blink at him. Interesting summary. Oddly, his words settle around me with a comforting sort of thud.

He cocks his head. "You wanna make this work, right?"

I open my mouth, taken aback by the redirect on my angst. It's all still sitting there in my chest, but it stopped simmering. Stopped churning. *"Yes,"* I snap, even though he doesn't deserve my anger.

"Hey." He brings one hand to settle on my waist. It does jumpy things to my insides, especially considering how on edge I am. "You're worried. I get it. But you have choices."

I find myself drifting closer to him, like the strength in that rock-solid body or his cock-sure attitude will magically transmit to me. "What choices?"

He shrugs. "You can keep worrying and do the same thing you've been doing."

I scowl, my lungs tightening again.

"Or you can start trying new things to grow your business. Because that's what you want, right? To grow it?"

I nod. Yeah. That's what I'd imagined when I decided to buy. I didn't picture myself just maintaining things the way Mary Alice had done them for years, and I definitely didn't think I'd have even less business than she had.

"I can't grow it when I have no money to invest. I mean, I couldn't even get the van fixed to keep deliveries going. That's why I've just been stuck treading water since I bought it."

"Then you figure something out."

I blink up at him. "Seriously? That's your advice?"

"Not every idea costs money. And money doesn't only come from one source."

I shake my head. I don't know why I thought he had some magic answers for me here. "What do you know, anyway?" I mutter, turning away.

He catches my arm and pulls me back. "Either give it up or fight for it, Flowers. Don't hold your breath and pretend it's not sinking when it is."

I'm not the type to get physical with anyone, but I give his chest a hard shove. "Fuck you, Armando."

I know, not a really profound comeback. But I—

I lose my train of thought when he captures my wrists and backs me into the wall, his hard body pressed against mine. "Watch it, Flowers."

I don't know why I get wet every time he manhandles

149

me. Or threatens me. It's like my body can't distinguish his abuse from foreplay. Not that it feels like abuse. His actions definitely read more as foreplay—it's not just me.

"Get off me," I whisper, but I clearly don't mean it.

"Breathe, Flowers."

I attempt to pull my wrists free, but he tightens his hold. "Breathe, or I'll make you."

"How will you do that?" I challenge. I'm way more turned on than afraid. I want all of his attention on me. On my body.

Maybe even on my business, even though he pissed me off.

He moves quickly, covering my mouth and nose with his free hand, blocking my air.

Surprise and fear leap to the surface, and I fight him, my survival instincts all kicking in.

He releases my wrists and shifts his other hand between my legs, cupping my mons firmly. He lets me take a quick breath, then smothers me again. Shock, terror and pleasure mingle in a rage of sensations. Blood rushes to my clit, tingles start up everywhere. He rubs firmly between my legs the whole time I freak out about not being able to draw a breath.

Just when I'm frantic, he pulls his hand away from my mouth and closes it around my throat instead. I suck in gasps of breath. It's only been thirty seconds, and I'm on the cusp of an orgasm. He doesn't choke me, he just uses his hand at my throat to hold me pinned against the wall while he works his fingers over my folds. He's not even inside me, and I'm ready to go. I reach down and cover his hand with my own, pushing his fingers more firmly against my clit, my entrance, my anus.

He grins and nods, his eyes glittering with pleasure as

my breathing grows more shallow. His other hand slides up my body, tracing a path up my neck and sending shivers through me, before coming to rest on my jaw. He looks into my eyes, and I can see the intensity in his gaze.

"I could fuck you all day, every day," he whispers, and I can feel his breath tickle my skin. I nod, unable to find the words.

He tightens his grip around my throat and leans in, pressing his lips to mine hungrily. His tongue explores my mouth, tasting and teasing, and my arousal grows.

With a growl, he slides two fingers inside me. I gasp at the sudden pleasure as he strokes, pushing his wrist against my clit as he does. He starts to move faster and harder, stimulating me in ways I didn't know could happen so closely to sex and being more than satisfied.

We just had sex.

Not being able to get enough of this man, I writhe and squirm against him, desperate for more. He takes up my challenge, alternating between hard thrusts and gentle caresses, driving me closer and closer to the brink of ecstasy.

He responds to my moans, pushing deeper and faster with each stroke. I can feel his breathing hitch as I mewl and pant against him, my body trembling with pleasure. His other hand slides around my waist, pulling me closer, and his tongue finds its way into my mouth, tasting and exploring me as his fingers move faster and faster over my sensitive skin.

The sensations are overwhelming. Every nerve is on fire, and I'm close to the edge, my hips bucking against his hand in a desperate attempt to reach climax—again. He must feel it too, and his tongue moves more fiercely against my own, his fingers working harder and harder until I can't take it anymore, and I scream out my release, my body shaking and shuddering.

As I come, choking and gasping for my breath, Armando keeps rubbing between my legs. Stars dance before my eyes, and I close them, shuttled away in some other universe.

When I come back to reality, when my breath slows, and I open my eyes, I find Armando leaning his forehead against the wall beside my head, stroking my jaw with his thumb. His fingers still wrap around my neck and stroke between my legs.

A full-body shudder runs through me, another release.

"Don't give up, Flowers. Stop holding your breath. You can fix this."

I sag against his body. "How?" I warble. I sound pathetic. I should be pissed over what he just did to me. Even if I liked it, it was high-handed and scary. I should push him away and tell him never to touch me again, especially in my place of business.

Instead, I fall into his arms and let him hold me up.

"You try every idea you have until something takes hold. Ask for help. Keep working it. You can do this. You're good at what you do. Trust in that."

As far as motivational speeches go, it's pretty flimsy, but I do strangely feel better. That's probably just the orgasm talking.

I push away from him, even though I'm not sure my legs will hold me. "You're still an asshole," I mutter.

"Believe it," he confirms as I walk away on shaky legs but *breathing* much better than before.

Looking over my shoulder, I catch the way his eyes watch every single move I make. He's hunting, and I'm an easy prey.

I could run. I should run. But with the way he watches over me, I'd surely trip on my lust and desire for this man and fall flat on my face. But then knowing Armando, he'd simply pick me up, smack my ass for trying to flee and fuck me all over again.

Chapter Twenty-Two

Armando

Hannah's all discombobulated. I can't decide if she's still mad at me or just in a post-orgasmic brain-fuck. She moves restlessly around the shop, randomly stopping to stare at her products but not getting anything done. I suppose it could be a business-related brain-fuck.

The door opens, and a tall young woman with bleach-blonde ringlets and freckles across her nose breezes in. "Sorry I'm late." She heads straight past the counter into the area where I'm lounging and drops her purse on the desk beside me. "Hi."

Whatever softening effect Hannah's had on me doesn't apply to her. I'm suddenly cold and hard again, showing nothing, ready for anything. I don't answer, other than to flick my brow in question.

It makes her nervous, and she backs out and cozies right up to Hannah. "What's with Guido?" I hear her murmur.

Hannah shoots a frightened glance at me, and I instantly prickle with irritation although I can't put my finger on why. I guess I don't like seeing that look on

Hannah's face, even when I'm the cause of it. "That's, ah, Armando," Hannah answers. "He's hanging out today."

"Why?" the woman demands. I can't tell if she works here or is just a friend. Possibly both.

"Armando, this is Josie," Hannah says in a louder voice. "She works here."

I glance at the clock. The shop opened at noon. It's 1:45 now. What time was she supposed to be here?

"Oh my God, were you not able to make the rent?" Josie whispers.

Hannah flicks another worried glance my way. "Not quite, but it's okay, I have things worked out for this month."

"What does that mean?"

Hannah just shakes her head. "Can you handle the counter?"

Josie gives her a searching look, but when Hannah ignores it, she says, "Of course."

Hannah buzzes past me and goes to her workbench. She pulls out a vase and two spools of ribbon. Now, she finally has focus. I realize she was waiting for someone to run the front desk, so she could get busy with the arrangements. I probably could have kept an eye on things. It's telling that she didn't ask me. I think she pretends to be more comfortable with me than she really is.

A stab of guilt shoots through me. The same shame I felt last night thinking she might believe she has to fuck me to stay alive.

Is she that good of an actress?

No. I don't think so. She's into it. Her body can't lie. She's not resisting me. Although...am I giving her much of a choice?

Hannah looks calm and confident, assembling buckets of flowers at her feet from the cooler. Where she might be a deer in the headlights when it comes to her books, here at the workbench, she's a goddamn wizard. Her movements are swift and sure as she fills it with a perky bouquet of colorful flowers and wraps a red and white ribbon around a vase. I don't even know what kind they are—orchids maybe? Something exotic and surprising. There's nothing cliche about the arrangement.

And then it hits me. "Is that supposed to be a barber's pole?"

She steps back, examining her work with a critical eye. "Yes."

Genius. Her talent as a designer is fucking off the charts.

"Did Rocco ask for flowers?" Funny, I can't see it.

"No. But he's getting them. I was thinking about what you said. About making new connections. You're right—I don't have any. And the only one Mary Alice had that still works for me is Rocco's. So I figure I should keep that wheel greased. From now on, Rocco's going to have fresh flowers at his place with a stack of my cards beside them."

"Smart thinking." I want to go over with her—watch how it goes down. I don't know if it's to protect her from the guys who might be over there or to stake my claim, but it doesn't matter because I can't.

Best way to protect Hannah is to never connect the two of us.

I gotta sit in the back of her shop like a fucking pansy, hiding from God knows who.

This is bullshit.

"You didn't tell me you had a staff person coming in today." I glance over at Josie who doesn't seem to be doing anything other than picking at her manicured nail and yawning as she does so.

"Her schedule can be...fluid," Hannah says, still focused on arranging.

She pulls another vase down and makes a bigger, showier arrangement in it. It's two feet tall and stunning.

"Who's that for?" I ask.

She nibbles her lip. "There's a hotel a couple blocks from here." She shrugs. "Maybe I'll go introduce myself. You know, in case they need flowers for events. Or could recommend me to the event-planners."

"That's good."

Maybe she will turn this place around.

"I'll drive you after we get the van back. Circle around the block, so you don't have to do valet."

She gives me a withering look. "I wasn't going to do valet. I've never done valet in my life. I was going to walk."

I look at her wedge sandals. "Nah. I'll drive you. You wouldn't want the flowers to wilt. Just wait for the van...it'll be done in a couple hours."

She draws in a breath and lets it out slowly, like she's nervous about this.

"You're gonna be great. They'll love you."

"You think?"

I nod. "Positive."

She steps a little closer to me, into my personal space. I only resist touching her until I realize that's what she wants, and then I band an arm around her waist and draw her right up against me.

She tips her lovely face up. "I'm nervous."

"Flowers, a woman who looks like you? With crazy talent and no diva bullshit? There's no one in this city who *wouldn't* want to work with you. I guarantee it. It's just gonna be about who they currently do business with and what their needs are. Some connections may take longer to germinate, but they eventually will."

She blinks those curled lashes at me. "I want to believe you."

"Don't believe me, Flowers. Believe in *you*. That's the only thing that will get you there."

She draws herself up and squares her shoulders. "Who do you believe in?"

It's a simple question. Should be an easy answer, but I feel like I've swallowed lead. "Nobody, Flowers. Not a Goddamn soul."

Chapter Twenty-Three

annah

Josie keeps trying to get me alone, but Armando won't let it happen. He appears deceptively relaxed, lounging around in the back, but he picked a spot where he can keep an eye on everything—front door, back door. Workshop. Coolers. Kitchenette. It's not like the shop is that big, but there's nowhere I go I don't feel the weight of his gaze.

And every time Josie tries to follow me somewhere with a million questions in her eyes, Armando's suddenly standing there, warning me without saying a word.

Right now, I'm in the cooler, but when Josie came in after me, Armando propped the door open, so he could hear.

It's freaky. It shouldn't get me wet. I'm not sure why his brand of intimidation turns me on so much. I must be wired wrong.

But Josie's concern makes my stomach knot up. I should've been more freaked out about Armando and my situation, but until now, when I see it through her eyes, I didn't realize how fucked up it is.

And of course, I can't tell her the situation. Even if Armando wasn't watching, I wouldn't tell.

I don't know, I'm one of those hopelessly loyal people who takes my friends' secrets to the grave. And I guess Armando falls into the friend category. He was already in it when the situation went down. I was rooting for him from the beginning.

I believed in him. He just doesn't believe in me yet.

I wish that didn't hurt as much as it does.

But I have to cut him slack. He probably has PTSD from prison. Someone's trying to kill him, and he doesn't know who to trust.

Why would he have any faith in me? He shouldn't.

I hear the sound of my phone chiming like I got a text. Repeatedly.

Where is my damn phone? Armando has it somewhere. He's kept it on him the whole time although I appreciate the fact that he made sure to charge it.

I look through the glass and see Josie behind the counter holding her phone and craning her neck to look over her shoulder at me. We've been besties since middle school when she stood up for me against Erica Bane, one of the popular girls, on the third day of school. She knows me through and through. I am stupid to think I can fool her about anything.

She's texting me. And she just realized I'm not in possession of my own phone.

This could be a problem.

I breeze out of the cooler like I own the place, which, funnily enough, I do. Too bad I never feel like it. "Have you seen my phone?" I ask Armando sweetly.

"Uh huh. You left it here." He hands it over, cool as a cucumber. I am slightly disturbed at how convincing he is. How smoothly he covers the lie. But he is a member of an organized crime family after all. And probably grew up in it.

I check the messages, which are all from Josie asking if I'm okay, whether she should go get help and WTF is going on.

Everything's fine, I text back. *I hooked up with him, and now he's hanging out. He helped pay the rent.* I make a point of letting Armando read over my shoulder before I send it.

All of that is true. Except maybe not the *everything's fine.*

I haven't forgiven him for tying me up last night. That piss-off still lingers, but otherwise...I am fine. Armando makes me nervous, but half that is the excitement of having him near. Watching me. Not knowing what he's going to do next.

Do I think he'll bury me in Lake Michigan when it's all done? No. I can't see it.

I may be shitty at business, but I'm empathic. I can't help but understand people because I feel their emotions as my own. At least that's how it feels. Josie thinks I'm nuts every time I tell her that, but I swear it's true.

I don't sense menace from Armando toward me. He gives off very little emotionally unless I count lust. But he's not evil. He's not planning my demise.

Josie: *You hooked up with him? Who is he? A complete stranger!!! I've never seen him inside the store before.*

Me: *He's that man I was telling you about from when I worked under Mary Alice. He came back into the store yesterday near closing time.*

Josie: *To buy flowers for his fiancée? Please tell me you aren't fucking a taken man. Hannah!!*

Me: *He's not with her anymore. They broke up years ago.*

I almost add that he just got out of prison, but don't feel it's any of Josie's business. Plus, I think she'd judge not only him but me for hooking up with a criminal. I'm not in the mood to defend my actions.

Josie: *Well... was the sex hot? Did it live up to the fantasy?*

I feel my face heat and steal a peak at Armando who is watching me but no longer trying to read my texts. I seem to have at least earned that small level of trust from him.

I keep trying to prove he can trust me, so he'll set me free, but if I were totally honest with myself, I'd have to admit I'm not ready for it to be over. I like the tingle of excitement I get knowing he's watching my every move. Remembering how much he appreciates my body. I might even be addicted already to the way he touches me.

Me: *So hot.*

Josie: *But why is he here?*

Me: *He's protective, I guess...*

Josie: *Okay, that is super hot. Protective, possessive...yes!*

Me: *You have no idea.*

Chapter Twenty-Four

Armando

After Hannah brings the flowers by the hotel and leaves her card, I pull in at a grocery store. I need a razor, toothbrush, and some other odds and ends. Plus, she has no food at her place.

"What are we doing?" Hannah asks.

"Getting groceries." I turn off the van and climb out, looking around to make sure no one's watching us. I haven't seen anything suspicious today, but I'd be stupid to get complacent. "Let's go."

She hops down and comes around.

"Stay close. Follow directions. Show me I can trust you."

She lets out a little huff of indignation. If she was going to try something, she would've done it a long time ago. I know that. But I don't trust anything anymore.

"Get a cart."

She shoots me a withering look. "Are you going to tie me to it, too?"

My dick twitches at the thought. "Don't tempt me, Curls."

"Oh, is it Curls now? I thought I was Flowers."

I ignore her, mostly because I'm way over my daily quotient on words. My throat is literally scratchy from talking so much today. Hooking my fingers around the front of the cart, I lead her toward the toiletries aisle. I find a toothbrush and toothpaste and a bag of razors. When I toss the box of condoms in the cart, she takes notice.

"You're just assuming we are going to have sex again? What if I want to go back to my no sex rule?"

"Okay."

"Why do you say *okay* like you don't believe me?"

I stop the cart and turn to face her. She's so damn beautiful, even when she's snippy. "Take it easy, Flowers. I'm gonna respect your decision on whatever you want in that regard."

That doesn't calm her down. In fact, she gives the cart a push, forcing me to move out of the way or get hit. I walk beside the cart as she marches down the aisle. "So, what are the condoms for? Are you going back to your strip club? Hmm? Going to pick up some girls there?"

Aw, fuck. I swear my face is breaking because I sense a smile coming on. Is she jealous? She's fucking adorable when she's jealous.

I stifle the smile and keep my face blank. "No. Not going back to the strip club, Flowers. They're in case you do decide you want to continue having sex with me."

She stops the cart and looks at me, considering. Her lips are in a pout, but her posture has softened. "I'll think about it."

I shrug. "Okay."

A blush spreads across her cheeks, and she starts

pushing the cart again at a determined speed. "What else are you getting?"

"Food."

"I need kitty litter," she mutters.

"Let's get some." We head to the pet aisle. She picks out the kitty litter. I throw in some Kitten Chow, and catnip treats and one of those poles with feathers attached to the end for the kitten to play with.

"I didn't think you liked cats." Hannah eyes me from under a swath of curls.

For some reason, it hurts that she noticed. That I can't hide my lack of humanity. "I don't," I say gruffly.

It's not true. I don't like or dislike cats. I don't give a shit about them. But I know it's fucked up that I can look a kitten in the face right now and feel nothing. There's definitely something wrong with me. All mammals are wired to think baby animals are cute. I learned that in middle school science class.

I stalk through the store. I picked up a few things at the grocery store before I moved into the apartment Marco rented for me, but I was in culture shock then. Just being in the grocery store had been an out of body experience—like most everything this past week. Now, I'm determined to find something I like or want. I drag Hannah through every aisle filling the cart with all kinds of food. Steak. Ice cream. Potato chips. Fresh fruit and vegetables. Oreo cookies.

"You'd better be paying for all this because I'm not," Hannah mutters when the cart gets full.

"Yeah, I got it."

After a few moments, she says, "I'm sorry—that was bitchy."

Seriously. This girl. Who does that? Who apologizes for an offhanded dig?

"Nah, you earned it."

"Well, I don't like the way it feels."

She doesn't like the way it feels. Hannah Munn is so pure, it makes my head spin. She's not innocent or naive. Not a mouse. She's just... kind. Good. Honest.

And she feels bad now because bitchiness is not her natural state. Grace could pull a cunt all day long and would never apologize for it. Hannah didn't even come close to offending me, and she can't let it ride.

"It was uncalled for. You helped me with money at the bank and with the van." Her voice breaks a little.

Aw, shit, is she crumpling? Over this?

"Come here, Flowers." I pull her against my chest and wrap my arms around her. "It's all right. It's just money. You gotta get over your fear of it."

"I'm not afraid of money," she says, sounding even more upset. She pushes out of my embrace, and I let her go.

"You might not be afraid, but it's your sore spot, for sure. You get more upset about money than you do about anything. Even what happened yesterday."

"Well, it's a big deal," she snaps.

"It's not. You've made it a big deal. It's just money."

"Have you ever not had enough?" she demands.

My memory flashes back to my teen years. My first job for Don G., providing security at Lollipops at age sixteen. Flexing my muscles and pretending to play hero to a bunch of naked girls. I got a taste for cash. Seeing the guys flash it around, going home with a wad of it in my pocket. Buying groceries and gas for my mom. Telling her to quit her second job. "I always wanted more," I admit. "That's how I got into the organization."

Her eyes widen, and she goes quiet, chewing on that. "Are you ever sorry?"

I let out a snort. Am I? I'm not even allowed to think it. I can't think it because if I do, there's no reason to go on living.

Once you're in, you don't get out, except in a body bag.

"Officially, no."

"Unofficially?" she asks softly.

"I have some regrets," I admit. "But there's no exit ticket. I'm in it for life now." I shrug. "I gotta make it work."

She blinks those curled lashes at me, seeing so much more than I want to show.

I gotta change the topic. "Come on, Flowers. Groceries are on me, so finish filling up this cart. I don't know what you like."

"Lobster and caviar, it is." She tosses her hair and swishes her hips as she pushes the cart down the aisle.

That twitchy feeling returns around my mouth.

A smile. Hannah makes me want to smile.

"If my princess wants lobster, then lobster it is," I say.

She pauses, nibbles her bottom lip, and then reaches for a box of plug-in air fresheners. "I'd prefer these over lobster. Help with the kitty smell. They're just super expensive for some oil you plug into the wall. But—"

I snatch them from her hand, not even looking at the price. "You're a cheap date."

She smiles again—a smile I could look at all day every day—and continues toward the check out.

We walk outside, and the thump of bass assaults us from a Chevy Impala low-rider. I whirl to face Hannah, catching the cart to stop it and her.

"What?" Her eyes widen. She's smart enough to recognize my urgency and scans the street, following the vehicle with her gaze. "You know them?"

I don't turn, even though I want to. I fucking hate

169

having my back to danger. "I don't know," I mutter. The pounding music fades.

"It's gone," Hannah tells me.

I turn back to the van and tug the cart, resuming like nothing happened.

Fuck.

That could've been the Hermanos. They could've had assault weapons and fired from the car. Hannah would've been killed.

I'm still ice-cold and emotionless when I picture myself getting gunned down, but the thought of Hannah dying because of me brings bile to my mouth.

I shouldn't be hiding out with her. It would be better to expose myself to danger than to use her as my shield.

I need to get out of her life.

Fucking soon.

Ushering her to the passenger side of the van, I open the door and assist her inside, feeling as if eyes are still on me. Watching my every move. I notice that Hannah is examining my face, obviously picking up on my discomfort. Not saying anything to explain, I close her door and walk around the van pissed that I let my guard down. My eyes dart from side to side, scanning the parking lot, and finally acting like the man I was trained to be.

No more playing house. Our fucking lives are on the line.

Chapter Twenty-Five

H*annah*

Shadow races to greet us when we get home, climbing Armando's pant leg.

"What the fuck?" He rears away to stare down his leg at my tiny sharp-clawed nuisance.

"I'm sorry." I rush over to extricate the kitten's claws from his thigh. "He's a menace."

"Let me see him." Armando holds out his hand. I hesitate a moment before I hand him over. I'm not sure where Armando falls with treatment of animals although he did buy toys for Shadow.

He takes Shadow from me and holds him up face-level. "Listen, little man. My leg? Not your scratching post. Got it?"

I giggle and reach to take him back.

"Give him one of those treats," Armando says, and my heart does this weird squeezing thing. Like we're pet parents together or something stupid like that. It's ridiculous and weird and *God*—this whole situation exhausts me.

I retrieve the treats and feed Shadow one while Armando puts away the groceries and sets the table.

I'm mad at him, I remind my ovaries, which drop eggs every thirty seconds. *Mad at him.* He tied me up in my own bed last night. He's taken my phone, which I *need.* He's still standing guard over me like I'm a prisoner.

Technically, I am a prisoner. Or am I? It's hard to feel like a prisoner when I keep fucking my jailer. I'm struggling to keep my hands off him right now.

We sit down and eat one of those pre-cooked rotisserie chickens and a Caesar salad that Armando made. Armando eats fast, head down, not saying a word. I picture him eating like that in prison, and my chest gets tight. I want to ask about it, but he's so closed off, I don't dare.

He finally looks up, pauses mid-chew, and swallows hard. As if it's just dawned on him that we've sat here in silence as he shoveled food into his mouth like a guard is waiting to take his tray away.

"So tell me something about you," he says.

"Um... like what?"

He pauses, his eyes dart around the room and then center back on me. "What is your favorite flower? I know you are around them all day and know the preferences of your clients. But what is yours?"

"Do I have to have one?"

"Yes. Everyone has a favorite."

"I guess... I like roses," I say. "Red ones." I'm not sure if I would have said that answer if I wasn't put on the spot.

"I would have guessed that," he says. "You have the personality of a rose."

My breath catches in my throat. "And what's that?"

"Strong, beautiful and demands attention."

"I don't demand attention," I say, surprised by his words.

"You should." He pins me with a gaze that makes my tummy flutter. "Never settle for anything else."

"What about you?" I ask. "Do you have a favorite flower?"

"Whatever one makes you happy. That would be mine."

He doesn't smile. He doesn't say the words in a way meant to charm me or woo me. They are simple, direct, and silencing. I don't know how to respond to this man.

So instead, I continue eating, as does he. Though we say very little, I'm comforted by his presence and the sound of his knife and fork against the plate. I shouldn't be reading into his words or his actions, and yet, I can't help myself.

When we finish, he helps me clean up just as efficiently as he does everything. It's like we're playing house, standing side by side washing dishes and putting them away. The only sound in the room is the running water and the meows of Shadow begging for chicken scraps.

I'm surprised when Armando kneels down and gives the cat a bite from his fingers. "That's it for now. It's rich," he says to the kitten as Shadow licks every last bit of juice from Armondo's beefy fingers.

He then takes his toothbrush and other toiletries off the counter and heads to the bathroom. I'm left feeling... odd. I don't know how to process everything going on and the rush of emotions both good and bad flowing through me. But I need to find my phone. I might have messages that need answering. I can't stand that he won't give it to me.

I search the high cupboards because that's where he stowed my purse last night. No dice.

Then I see it. It's on top of the refrigerator, pushed way

to the back behind the floral baskets I have stacked there. It amuses me that he hides it up high. Like I'm some little girl who can't reach.

Okay, actually, I can't reach because I'm short, but I put one knee up on the counter and reach. I fish out my phone and check the texts.

There's two. One from my mom, asking if I'm coming to dinner tomorrow, and one from Josie, telling me she'll be late Monday.

Not asking. *Telling.*

Sigh. Another problem I'm sticking my head in the sand about.

I start to reply when I hear Armando curse.

He storms at me, but I don't flinch. Yes, he's capable of hurting me. He's violent. Dangerous. But there's thought and control behind the violence. And I'm fairly certain he has rules about hurting women. As in, he won't. And frankly, if he was going to hurt me, he would have done it by now.

"What the fuck, Hannah?" he snatches the phone out of my hand, his brows in a deep V as he scrolls over my screens. "Who did you message?"

"*Nobody.*" I let my irritation show. I lift my chin at the phone. "Check it yourself."

His thumb flies over the screen as he checks my phone log, too. "You could've sent one and erased it."

"I need my fucking phone, Armando." I let myself sound bitchy because it's a better alternative to allowing him to bully me or showing fear.

He shakes his head and shoves the phone in his back pocket. "That's not how this works, and you know it, Flowers." He catches my wrists and pins me with a dark gaze. "I trust you and leave for one minute... And now you're in big trouble with me."

Big trouble.

Why does that make my belly flip flop with excitement?

Because I already know I like his punishments. He spins me around and slaps my hands on the refrigerator, then pulls my hips back to bend me at the waist. My wrists are manacled under one of his meaty palms.

I'm prepared for the slap when it comes, but it's harder than I expect, and I gasp. He smacks my other butt cheek just as hard, then yanks my minidress up to my armpits. He spanks my ass some more over my panties.

"Ow, okay," I snap because it really does hurt.

He brings his mouth close to my ear—close enough that his warm breath feathers across my jaw when he speaks. "You keep your hands glued to that fridge, Hannah," he warns. "If you move, I will make you sorry."

He doesn't wait for my agreement but releases my wrists to yank my panties down my thighs.

Oh God.

It's so hot but also borderline humiliating. Especially because they tangle around my thighs and stay there. I wiggle and shake my legs until they fall down.

"Good girl," Armando says, and everything shifts.

Maybe I had been a little afraid up to that moment. He was a little rougher than he's been in the past. Spanked a little harder. Now I'm sure of him again.

"I'm not having sex with you," I say, trying to maintain the one level of control he's given me.

Sex is the only leverage I have—not that he couldn't just force me. But I know he won't.

"Understood, but that's not gonna stop your punishment." His voice is deep and gruff.

Well, good. I didn't particularly want to stop my punishment. Except he picks up spanking me again, and it's still too hard.

"Ouch!" I jerk and wince as he peppers my ass with five more hard spanks.

"And there is so much I can do to you besides just fucking you."

He continues to spank me more. My ass getting warmer with each swat of his hand. What hurts also feels so fucking good.

"Are you going to be a good girl and follow my rules? Or do I need to keep spanking you?" His voice is deep, authoritative, and my pussy pulsates with each syllable of his question.

"I'll be a good girl." Even though I'm saying the words, they seem to vanish, drowning between my gasps and mewls.

"Do you want Daddy to punish you like a naughty girl or punish you like the bad girl you are?"

Holy. Fucking. Christ. His one question is like a bolt of electricity zipped through me. So fucking intense.

"I want both, *Daddy*." I inhale deeply. "Both."

Then he drops to his knees behind me and pinches my asscheeks with his thumbs. He pulls them apart and licks up my crack.

I let out a warble of pleasure. God, yes. Wherever this man learned to fuck, he learned it right.

He rims my anus with his tongue, then pushes my thighs wider to open me to him. Face buried in my ass, he licks up to my clit and back again. The sting of his spanks morphs into a warm tingle, bringing added heat to the region, as if my core weren't already molten.

He slaps my ass intermittently as he works my folds

with his tongue, then screws one finger into me. His thumb rubs over my anus.

"Good thing we're not having sex, Flowers. Or I'd bend you over, put my cock in your ass and fuck you hard."

Oh. My. *Gawd*.

Armando shifts to dip his thumb in my pussy, then returns to my anus with it coated with my juices and pushes like he's trying to get in. He puts three—fuck, maybe four—fingers in my pussy at the same time.

I do scream—a loud, "Oh my God!" I lose my balance, my knees buckling. Armando grips my pelvis to hold me up and removes his fingers. "No," I whimper. Dammit. I was so close to coming.

He grabs me around the waist and pulls back. I shriek as I free-fall into his lap, but he doesn't miss a beat. He hooks his hand behind my left knee and pulls it up and open, spreading me wide. With his right palm, he starts *spanking my pussy*.

Quick firm slaps. He slaps everything—my clit, my entrance, my labia. I wriggle in his lap, trying to push him away at the same time I pull him closer. It's crazy intense. Like lose-my-mind intense in a really good-bad way. Hurty but really freaking satisfying.

I shriek and grab the hand spanking me, cup it around my mons, so I can come. He curls his fingers and dips them in—two, maybe three—and I come, a spasm of release rippling through me.

"Oh fuck," I pant. "Oh my God."

I come some more.

He undulates his hand, so the heel of it pulses against my clit. I come again.

"Jesus." I fling myself back into his arms, my head lolling over his shoulder.

He pulls his fingers out of me, and I moan, but he gives my pussy three more quick slaps, and I come again.

"Holy freaking shit," I pant. "What in the hell did you just do to me?" My whole body is abuzz, ass tingling, pussy raw and sore from the spanking, anus still pulsing from being breeched.

I turn my face into his neck because my eyes suddenly burn with the release. I know if I don't make anything of it, the emotions will pass through me, but I don't want him to see. It's so weird how easily I cry.

He shifts my ass to hold me better, and I feel his rock-hard erection prod my butt. I don't feel guilty. Not really.

But the truth is, I'm still revved up. I don't know, maybe my body's not quite satisfied until I go the whole way. Until I actually ride his cock.

"The only way I'd have sex with you would be if I tied you up this time," I tell him.

"Not gonna happen," he answers without hesitation, but I feel his cock lurch against my backside. He brings his fingers to my clit and rubs a slow circle.

Shit!

This man's touch is my kryptonite. I swear he could make me do anything if he just made me come this hard every day.

I put my face back in the crook of his neck and whimper. I may have just come, but the need is still there. And he's amping it up with every rub of my clit.

"I'd let you ride me no-hands," he offers.

I bite his neck because I'm frustrated. "What is that?"

"You know. Like at a strip club. You can climb all over me, but I can't touch you."

He had to bring up strip clubs and remind me of last night. "No, I don't know. I've never been," I say tartly.

"You wanna ride my cock?" He massages a handful of my ass.

Unfortunately, it seems my body wants nothing more. It holds no grudges.

When I hesitate, he moves, lifting me off his lap and pulling me to my feet as he stands. Then he swings me up into a baby carry. I gasp, worried I'm too heavy, but he doesn't appear to be straining.

And being carried is a delicious feeling. One I don't want to indulge in because there are already way too many things about the way Armando touches me I like. I don't want to get used to any of it because it's not a relationship. It's not permanent. It's this weird high-stress shared experience that forged intimacy. Like people who band together during the zombie apocalypse and are forced to develop bonds that would never exist otherwise.

And yeah, it says something that I'm comparing our situation to the one faced by the characters in *The Walking Dead*.

He sets me on my feet near the bed and pulls my dress, which is still tangled up around my armpits, over my head.

I give his chest a light push, which of course, doesn't move him at all. "No touching," I remind him.

Chapter Twenty-Six

Armando

Mary, Queen of Peace. I'm harder than stone for Hannah. What kind of magical creature is she to transform every conflict into explosive sex? She just fucking surrenders to me. Even when she wants to hold back, her body melts with my touch, all the dirty things I do to her. I don't plan to do them, but she makes me. She brings it out in me. Her body receives, and mine wants to give. It's impossible for me not to deliver every caress, every spank, every orgasm she seems to crave.

And right now she wants to pretend she has control, so I'll give it to her. I strip out of my clothes and grab a condom out of my wallet. I flop onto the bed on my back and roll the condom on my erection.

Hannah's ditched all her clothing. She's freaking glorious—all soft curves and dark skin with that insane mane of hair tumbling over her shoulders and down her back. She climbs onto the bed.

I tuck one hand behind my head but hold the base of

my cock with the other until she takes over. A shudder of pleasure runs through me the moment she fists it.

"I'll bet you want me to suck it," she says, pupils blown.

The erection punches out harder. "Fuck!"

"I'm not sure you deserve that." She's playing cock-tease, but I don't give a shit because she climbs over me and lines up that sweet pussy of hers with the head of my shaft. She rubs her juices over it, then sinks down.

I growl, barely stopping myself from reaching for her hips to help. It's fucking hard not to use my hands. Because she's not some stripper-stranger. She's Hannah, and I can't fucking wait to see her come all over my cock.

She rocks slowly over me, her pelvis undulating, her tits shifting. It's goddess worthy. I want to touch those juicy tits. I want to rub her clit. I want to yank her down on me so hard she sees stars. But she's got the control now. And I'm grateful as hell to be inside her.

I roll my hips in time with hers, shifting up to thrust into her when she rocks down. It quickly becomes too much for her. She braces her hands on my shoulders and starts riding me faster, her breasts swinging, hair falling in a curtain around my head.

I fist the pillow behind my head—tear at it—to keep from breaking my word not to touch. When she sees my dilemma, she pins my wrists down on the bed like I'm her prisoner and slides that magic pussy faster and faster over my cock. She works it and works it like a fucking Energizer Bunny until she runs out of breath from the exertion and stops moving, panting.

I lift my hips to meet her every downward thrust. It feels incredible. She's so wet and so tight. And when I look up, I see her tits bouncing and her nipples stiffening. There's no way I can keep my hands still for a few more seconds. They're itching to touch her. To squeeze the ripe mounds. To circle her stiff nipples with my thumb and forefinger. To slide to her clit and make her come.

I'm on the edge. Balls-deep in that slick cunt, backed up against her cervix, I work my hips to get even deeper. My fingers twitch.

She arches backward and clamps down hard on my cock. The shock of her pussy muscles contracting around me is almost enough to send me over. She's panting now, her tits bouncing as she grinds her pelvis forward and back.

I stretch my arms up and slide my hands up her body until they cup her breasts, squeezing and kneading them. Her eyes go wide, and she swallows. I drop one hand to rub her clit. I can't stop myself. I'm too close. Her hips buck against mine, fucking me. I move my thumb in a figure eight over her clit until she's moaning and begging for release.

I let go of her tit and grab her ass to bury myself in her as far as I can. Watching her arch back to meet me as she releases a raspy moan.

Fuck.

"Let me touch you," I start begging. "Let me drive, doll. I'll make you feel so good, I promise."

Her eyes are smoky, rose flushes her skin. She blinks those curled lashes at me as she considers. I thrust my hips up to get deeper and she moans.

The moment she gives me a minuscule nod, I wrap my fingers around her hips and start controlling the movement. I lift and lower her over me, thrusting my hips in time to meet hers. It feels like heaven, but I'm also getting desperate to finish. I've been hard for her all day and just watched her come on the kitchen floor.

She moans like she's getting close with the short, sharp cries that fall like music in the room.

We're both close, but it doesn't happen, and I think a change of position would help. "Let me put you on your back."

I'm not usually one to ask for permission for anything, but she's holding this power over me now, and I'm gonna let her. It's my penance. Better than the ones Father Fantoni assigns.

"Okay," she gasps.

I flip her around in one second flat, keeping our hips glued together. As soon as I'm on the top, I start thrusting with force. Hannah's eyes roll back in her head, her lips fall open with pleasure. She cups her own breasts. I hold the place where shoulder meets neck to keep her head from banging into the wall and fuck the living daylights out of her.

When I decide I need to be deeper, still, I lift one of her thighs up and pound into her in that position.

I kiss her hard again, one more time. This time, my tongue is forceful and dominant. I take her tongue and suck it hard into my own mouth, forcing her to submit. She's mine. She's going to remember that. I want to leave a mark on her. I want her to be able to smell me on her, feel me deep within her. I want her to think of me every time she touches herself or remembers this night.

"You taste so fucking good, Hannah. I'm going to make you come so hard. I'm going to make you scream."

I watch as she falls apart around me, her legs shaking and her back curling, her whole body holding the weight of an orgasm that is too intense. She breathes deeply and hard from her core, writhing against me, her hands holding on tightly to my forearms. Each time her body wraps around mine, I feel my own orgasm build.

"I'm going to come, baby," I growl. "I'm going to fill you up...."

She starts screaming, filling the room with ecstatic needy shrieks. My balls draw up tight, thighs shaking.

"Fuck, Hannah, I'm gonna come," I tell her as stars start to explode behind my eyes.

"Yes!" she cries. "Me too!"

Hannah's orgasm is so powerful, she's shaking even while mine rips through my body, taking over and shaking me to my core. I don't want to stop. I want to stay inside her forever, feel her body pull me deeper, keeping me here, connected.

I continue to come, still banging her hard, and she bites her lip, arches her back and screams some more. Her pussy contracts around my dick, pulsing and squeezing with her climax.

Christ, she's everything.

She really is.

I slow down and stroke slowly for a while, taking it down to a caress then finally stopping and feeling my cock pulse and twitch inside her with the aftershocks.

"*Bella.*"

She frowns and lifts her head from the pillow. "What?"

"You're beautiful."

"Did you just call me by another woman's name?" Her voice is sharp and offended.

A snort of laughter surprises me. Jesus. When's the last time I laughed?

"No, I said *bella*. It means *beautiful* in Italian." I ease out and pull off the condom, reaching behind me to drop it in the trash by the bed.

"Oh." She goes soft and receptive again. Fuck, I love

how receptive she is. I'm also loving her jealousy. "Do you speak Italian?"

I settle beside her and stroke my palm over her hip. "A little. I understand it better than I speak it. I'm second generation American, so my grandparents speak it."

"Wow." She turns into me, her palm coming to rest on my chest. "Are you always... like this?"

I push a swatch of curls over her shoulder, so I can see her gorgeous breast. "Like what?"

She chews her lip. "Like this in bed."

I only partially manage to hide my surprise. I learned a long time ago that any time you get a woman to talk about sex, you don't do anything to shut that communication down. Hannah wants to talk—I'm in. Even if I am so far out of touch with my emotions, I'm a robot.

I consider. "No. I don't think so. I used to have more game. My techniques were... more stylized. I even thought sophisticated. But with you..." I close my eyes letting pleasure of what we just did wash over me. "It's more raw. Hungry. Almost desperate."

She blinks at me. There's vulnerability shining in those sultry brown eyes, but I'm not sure what she needs me to say. Or if I already fucked this up.

"Every time we do it, something in me thaws," I admit.

More vulnerability washes over her face, and her breath quickens. Is her lower lip trembling?

I come out with it—all the honesty I know how to give. "You're healing me."

Her eyes fill with tears, and she lets out a puff of air. I cup her face, trying not to react to the tears. A couple spill down her cheek, and I thumb one away.

"You're *destroying* me." Her voice chokes with tears.

I freeze. Stop breathing.

What is she saying? What is she telling me here? Fuck.

That shifty thing happens again in my chest.

"How?" My whole body's tense for her answer.

She sits up, and I follow. "Armando, what is this? I don't even know what we're doing, but I know it's a bad idea."

Aw, shit. My heart stops beating. My chest goes stiff.

"I don't have the answers you're looking for," I admit.

"Everything is happening so fast. Like a raging storm."

"It is."

"So what is this? Is it just sex... a lot of it?"

I shake my head. "No, Flowers. It's not just sex. I can tell you that much." Although I can't keep my damn hands off this woman.

"But it's dangerous," she adds.

A fist clenches in my gut.

"I don't keep feelings locked up in a box. My emotions are big, and they bleed into everything. And I don't want to fall in the deep end when I know there will be no one around to pull me out."

I digest that metaphor. Does *the deep end* mean love?

Fuck.

I want to tell her I won't hurt her. But she's right. Someone wants me dead. I don't know if I'll live through the week. And even if I do, Hannah and I are worlds apart. She's color and light and delicate flowers.

I'm darkness.

Death.

Destruction.

I live and breathe in a den of sin.

I have zero to offer her.

In fact, my continued presence in her life is only a grave danger to her.

187

Alta Hensley & Renee Rose

As soon as I stop pretending I believe she's actually a problem for me, I should walk.

Walk away and never look back.

If I had any decency, I'd do it right now.

But I don't. I grip her face and claim her mouth like she just professed her love to me. Which, in a way, she did.

"We're both in the deep end, Flowers," I tell her when we break apart.

I've never been in so deep.

She bleeds.... I bleed.

Chapter Twenty-Seven

annah

HArmando's phone rings in the middle of the night. The way he rips out of bed on a gasp tells me he's used to waking up fighting. Another sharp inhale through his nose, and the light from his phone comes on. His expression is hard. Warrior-like. "Yeah?"

I hear a clipped male voice on the other line, the tone just as sharp as Armando's. I hear the words *shot up* and *cops.*

Armando swears and starts pulling on his clothes like he's going to battle. "'Kay. I'm coming down... No, I'll Uber... Yeah."

I turn on the bedside lamp and climb out of bed, too. My heart pounds, even though I don't know what the emergency is.

Armando ends the call and buttons his pants, then slides the phone in his pocket.

"What's the matter? Who was that?" I ask. Maybe I'm being too forward, but he is in my apartment and in *my bed.* I think I've earned the right.

He turns to look at me. His face is hard. Unforgiving. His expression is lethal.

"I need to leave." His eyes dart around the room. "You're going to have to stay—"

"Don't even think about tying me up." I'm proud of myself for keeping my voice low and threatening, instead of hysterical, like last time.

He *is* thinking about it. I can tell because he doesn't move. He's still standing there, looking at me.

"Don't. Armando, when are you going to trust me? I'm not going anywhere. I'm just going back to sleep."

He yanks open my drawer and pulls out a pair of my tights again. "I don't trust you, okay? *I don't. Trust.* Believe me when I say tying you up is better than what I'd have to do to just leave my message and walk away. There'd be no coming back from that."

His words sting. He can *fuck* me but not *trust* me.

"You won't come back from tying me up again either," I warn. I look around for a weapon. When I don't see a good one, I pick up the lamp. "I will fight you." I lift it up like I'm going to bash him with it. I probably couldn't bring myself to use it, especially because after seeing him fight in my shop, I know my chances of winning any battle with him are miniscule. And I'd probably get hurt— *ah.*

I remember his weak spot. "You'd have to hurt me." That would bother him. It's against his personal code.

Nothing changes in his face, and yet I somehow know I've won because he moves again, dropping the tights into the drawer and looking around for his keys. "Put the lamp down. Get in that bed." It's a sharp command.

I don't move.

His phone rings again. He looks at the screen, expression grim. "This is Armando....Yes, sir. Yeah, I already heard... No, I'm not in the vicinity, but I can be there in twenty minutes.... Okay, I'm coming now."

When he hangs up, he points a finger at me. "In the bed before I change my mind. I'm taking your phone and your iPad. If you open that front door, I will know, and there will be hell to pay when I get back. I'm saying this for your safety. *Capisce?*"

My heart pounds, but my ridiculous body is turned on by his bossiness. I climb in the bed, pleased with myself for successfully negotiating my freedom. If you count the sovereignty of my hands as freedom.

"What happened?" I ask, even though I know he won't tell me.

"Go back to sleep, Flowers."

"You can take the van," I offer. "Or I could drive you."

"I'm fine." His statement is firm, and I know there is no arguing. "What happens in my *life* can't involve you. Period."

I roll my eyes and wait, sitting up in bed, watching him leave. He starts out the door then comes back in, looking at me.

"Hey, listen..."

I wait.

"If I'm not back by morning, you can leave. Keep your mouth shut and go about your business like you never knew me. Okay?"

I stare at him, ice sluicing through my veins.

When I don't respond, he adds, "I mean it, Hannah. You never knew me. Never saw me. Nothing. Got it?"

He thinks there's a chance he might not come back. What does that mean? That he'll be dead? Or back in prison?

What in the hell is happening?

I'm suddenly terrified for him, but there's nothing to be said or done because he's already gone.

I sit in the lamp-light for a long time, my heart pounding for him.

Armando. Shit!

Why does it feel like life or death for me, too? I don't want to care this much. He's not my boyfriend. He's not even a friend. He's not anything. And yet I'm already fully invested. Same as ever—falling too fast. Too hard. Too intensely.

But knowing that doesn't change this crashing sensation all around me. Armando is mixed up in something bad. And I really don't want him to die.

But this is my reality if there is to be anything with this man. He's in the mafia. I know this. I can't ignore this. He is who he is, and I'm just a girl who owns a flower shop.

There's a wall built around him made from bricks of traditions, rules, dictates from people more powerful than he. It's a den of sins he lives in, and no matter how much I'm enjoying this little game of playing house with him, I need to remember my reality.

What if he doesn't come back?

What if he *does* come back?

Chapter Twenty-Eight

*A*rmando

Mother. *Fucker*.

My whole body's ice cold as I get out of the Uber in front of my apartment building. Four squad cars and an ambulance block the road, lights flashing. Cops crawl all over the place. I hold my hands in the air as I approach.

"I'm Armando Rossi, the guy whose apartment was shot up," I tell the first cop who spots me.

"All right." He speaks into his comm unit. "I've got the victim down here." He listens to the answer. "Yeah, I'll bring him up." He eyes me suspiciously. "You have any weapons on you?"

I keep my hands in the air. "No, sir."

He pats me down to be sure then cuts, "Come with me."

On my floor, I see Marco standing with an officer. His apartment is two flights up, next door to Leo's. I hope to God their places weren't involved in this shit too.

He lifts his chin at me. We pass the apartment manager,

who points and snarls, "I want you out of this place by tomorrow. I never should've let a felon rent here."

"He stays," Marco's firm but raised voice cuts across the low conversations going on, making everyone look.

I ignore them both. I'm dead again. I taste ash on my tongue. My movements are mechanical. I see in shades of dark grey. Everything closes around me like the metal bars of my cell back in Joliet. I could easily kill or be killed right now without a single emotion.

A police officer meets me at my door. "You Armando Rossi?"

"Yes, sir."

He looks at the officer who brought me up. "Has he been patted down?"

"Yes, sir, he's clean."

"Can I see some ID?"

I produce my wallet and the ID card I got last week, since my license has been revoked. He pulls out a notepad and pencil and copies down my information. "Can you tell me what happened here?"

I shake my head. "No, sir. I was away."

"What do you think happened?" he snaps, obviously irritated by me. He's already made some judgement about me, and I'm sure it wasn't generous.

"I think..." I look around at my apartment. There are bullet holes in every wall. The glass in the artwork Marco had hung is shattered, covering the floors. The flat screen is busted all to hell. A giant spider web of cracks run through the window that overlooks the street, but the glass hasn't fallen in or out.

Yet.

Fluff from the sofa pushes from the upholstery. Marco already told me what he heard and saw, so it's easy to picture it. Some guys busted in and fired hundreds of rounds from a semi-automatic weapon into my place. "I think someone wants me dead."

"Who?"

I shake my head immediately. "No idea."

He narrows his eyes. "Who would you guess?"

I shrug. "No idea."

"Landlord said you're just out of prison."

I should say, *yes, sir,* but I'm suddenly done with the fucking conversation. I want everybody the hell out. I need to talk to Marco and Leo. So I stare the asshole down. It wasn't technically a question, so I'm not going to deign to answer.

I clear my throat. "Can I look around?"

The cop narrows his eyes at me again. "You have anything worth stealing here?"

"No." I drop the *sir*. Like I said, I'm done.

He tucks his notebook and pencil back in his pocket. "Yeah. Look around, let me know if anything's missing."

I head into the bedroom. It looks just as bad as the living room. Bullet holes in the doors, the headboard. Feathers from the pillows strewn about the room. They probably started here. When they realized I wasn't home, they shot the place up anyway.

It's a message. They're coming for me.

This feels more like The Hermanos than the hit on Friday did.

I did stash some of that start-up cash the don gave me in the apartment, but I don't want to check with the cops here. I don't need to explain where I got seven large—what's left of the money after helping my ma and Hannah out. Marco wouldn't take any money for the deposit and rent he paid on this place nor for the furnishings he bought to fill it.

We stand around with our thumbs up our asses for another forty minutes before the boys in blue finally pack it up and leave. The landlord is still standing outside, waiting to confront me. Marco walks over to stand by my side.

"Listen," he says, spreading his hands in a conciliatory fashion. "I just can't have your type around here. My residents need to feel safe, and what happened tonight is going to kill my business."

There's a time I would've given shit back to him. I'm pretty fucking alpha dog, and I don't let anyone push me around. But at this moment, I just can't bring myself to give two fucks. I don't care if I stay in this apartment building or go. It's not like I've spent any time here to begin with since meeting Hannah.

I'm not even angry about what happened. There's no sense of vengeance ringing through me. No desire for retribution.

I'm just fucking dead again.

And that's really the only thing I find disturbing.

But then again, who gives a fuck? Because it's sort of an out-of-body experience.

But Marco, he gives all the fucks right now. He steps into the landlord's personal space, not touching, but getting right in his grill. "No, what would kill your business, friend, would be getting on the wrong side of the Pachino family. My cousin stays. I stay. My brother stays. And if you hassle any one of us again, I will fucking take this business down, along with you and everyone you care about." Marco steps back. "Believe it, old man."

The landlord believes it. He believes it so bad, his face turns white, and his goddamn teeth start chattering. And Leo, with impeccable timing, picks that moment to show up, his bulky mass adding to the threat.

"Now get out of our faces."

The landlord bolts.

Marco and Leo wait until he's gone before they push into my apartment. Marco's in his white undershirt and a pair of slacks, like he yanked them on when it happened. Leo looks like he took more time to get dressed. "Definitely the Hermanos," Marco says. "I saw the fuckers running to a car on the street. They wore ski masks and carried semis. I heard a cop say they shot out the cameras out front and the glass door. Then they just rode the fucking elevator up here and shot up your place. Did you tell Don G?"

"Not yet." I side-eye Leo because while he's also like a brother to me, the fewer people who know my shit, the better.

He produces a gun from his back waistband and ammo from his pocket. "I know you're not allowed to keep a gun but seems like you'd be safer with a piece on you at all times right now."

Maybe my soul hasn't completely shriveled because a thread of gratitude twirls through me. My family takes care of me. Through thick and thin.

I take the pistol and tuck it in the back waistband of my pants. "Yeah, thanks."

"I'm worried about your ma," Marco says. "If they didn't find you here, you think they'd look at her place for you?"

I scrub a hand across my face. "I had the same thought. I'll see if I can send her on a vacay."

I stalk to the bedroom to look for my cash under the bathroom sink. It's all still there. But I'm not surprised. This wasn't a robbery.

They were out for blood, for sure. And after making as much noise as they did, they had to get the fuck out fast.

Frankly, I'm surprised they risked it in an apartment building like this one.

I pull a duffle bag out of the closet and start throwing my clothes and shoes and toiletries in it. Hannah's apartment is still the safest place for me. My instinct to stay there was dead on. But Marco's right, my mom could be in danger. And that thought does make me feel. I'd do anything for my mom. Growing up, it was just the two of us, and I'd kill or die for her in a second.

"I'll get my crew over here to clean shit up tomorrow," Marco offers.

"Thanks."

"What else can I do?"

"Nothing. I already owe you. I don't like being so out of balance with you, man." I give him one of those dude handshake hugs and thump him on the back.

He pulls back and meets my gaze. He's got light green eyes the color of cash. Total lady killer. "You'd do it for me." His expression is dead serious like he's swearing a vow.

I realize then that he's not just taking care of family. And it's not just pity. He feels guilty I got caught. I took the fall, and he didn't. Leo didn't. The rest of our crew that ran the car heist operation didn't. I just had the shit luck of getting pinched. And it goes without saying, I kept my mouth glued shut.

I want to say something to let him off the hook. Because it's the same story—he would've done the same thing in my shoes. Maybe he's eaten up because of how far I fell. I was at the top of my game then. I thought I was in love. Engaged to a beautiful woman. Making money hand over fist. I'd gained recognition and respect within the organization. I led my own crew—Marco and Leo worked for me. I was poised to become a leader and move up through the ranks as the older generation retired.

And then my fence got pinched, and I showed up at his garage driving a brand-new, stolen Mercedes Benz at the wrong time. I got out and ran, but they cornered me, and it was done. All I could do was ride it out. Serve my sentence and restart.

Since words are no longer my thing, I choke on any sentiment and settle for a fist bump. I bump Leo, too. "You still have a key to my place, right?"

"Yeah, we got it. You wanna stay at my place tonight?" Marco asks.

"Nah. I got a place." I pick up my duffel bag and head for the door.

Marco gives me a searching look but doesn't ask where I'm sleeping. In our line of business, the less you know, the safer you are. I know Marco and Leo would never roll over on me, but I wouldn't want them to be in the position of keeping secrets for me. They already keep enough.

"Lie low, then."

"Yeah. I will. Thanks again." I touch the pistol at my back and nod at Leo.

"Wait, no fucking way am I going to just let you walk out that door without some eyes. Especially if there is a girl in the picture now," Leo says.

"I got it under control," I say.

"Leo's right," Marco says. "At least let us put a man on guard. Back up just in case."

I open my mouth to argue but then think of Hannah. Though I'm trying to lay low, there is a chance whoever wants me dead now knows about her. If not for me, then I should most certainly make sure there are always eyes on her. Nodding, I say, "Yeah, not a bad idea. I want Hannah safe."

"So she has a name," Leo says with a smirk.

I walk over to the disaster of a kitchen and find a notepad and pen in the drawer. I jot down the address to her apartment and to the Garden of Eden and hand it to Leo.

He looks at the address. "That florist next to Rocco's?"

I nod again. "I'll text you the info on her friend and staff person who works there as well. I'd like to make sure she's kept safe during this. I don't want her caught in the crossfire."

Marco looks over Leo's shoulder at the note, and adds, "Consider it done."

"We'll figure out who's responsible and put an end to it. Guaranteed," Leo promises.

My younger cousin became a man while I was away. I see a maturity in Leo that didn't exist before I went to prison.

A million small things changed while I was away. The changes seem subtle, yet it's enough to feel like an entirely different world.

Or maybe it's just me who is entirely different.

And if I want to live to see next week, I'd better figure my shit out, fast.

What's going on. What to do about it.

Who I can trust.

Who do I have to kill to stop the hits from coming my way.

And yet, it's still hard to get interested in solving my problems.

The only thing that remotely interests me right now is Hannah. I want to be sleeping in her bed right now.

I'm a greedy bastard.

I know I should leave her alone. I should stay the fuck away from her, especially considering the danger I bring to anyone around me.

But I can't.

She's my lifeline.

The only road lit up is the one to her right now.

The only path I see to get home.

Chapter Twenty-Nine

annah

I stare down at Armando's sleeping form in my bed. He came in close to dawn and has been crashed ever since. He's sprawled on his back, the sheet tangled around his waist. His lean, sculpted muscles make him appear dangerous even in sleep. Shadow is curled up and purring against his waist, an unlikely bed partner.

I don't see any blood, scrapes, or bruises on him, and it makes me think that this could become my new normal—scanning his body for damage. If Armando and I continue with whatever it is this is, him leaving in the middle of the night, and me wondering if he's going to make it home unscathed, this will be our life.

But can I handle it?

Can I handle *him*?

When he came in and crawled up behind me, I pretended to be asleep. I didn't know what to say or do. It's not like I could ask him how his day at work went. I couldn't tell him I spent the night on the verge of puking and crying. I was terrified of what could happen to him, and what would happen if he never walked back through that door. But as he spooned his warm body up against mine, wrapping his heavy arm around my frame, I felt safe. In fact, I never felt safer. The feeling he gave me that very second made it all worth it. It made *him* worth it.

I debate whether to wake him or let him sleep. I have to get to the shop. I don't know why I feel like I need to ask his permission to leave. Just because he considers me a prisoner doesn't mean I am.

Except I like being his prisoner. That's the foolish truth. I don't actually want him to set me free and walk away. Because I'm already falling hard for this guy. Just like I always do when I start sleeping with someone.

I don't know how to contain my emotions. How to hold them back. I love big, and it's always messy. It always scares the guy away.

Maybe that's why being a prisoner appeals to me. Armando won't scare off. He's forcing himself on me, not the other way around. I can't really screw this up because there's nothing to screw. It's not a relationship. I didn't choose it. I can't even un-choose it other than refusing to have sex with him—which I epically fail at doing.

And why would I do that? It's the best part of this situation. Although it's not just the sex I enjoy. I love the excitement. The edge of danger offset by a level of trust. Also, I like how he takes care of me in micro ways—like buying me food and taking out the trash. Cleaning up after meals. My life seems a little more manageable with someone looking out for me. Contributing. I'm so used to being the one worrying about everyone else, it's nice to have someone paying attention to me for a change.

I touch his hard biceps. "Armando?"

He sucks in a sharp breath, sitting bolt upright with a gun in his hand... aimed at me.

I yelp in surprise and freeze. I don't even know where the pistol came from—I have to replay the scene to realize he pulled it out from under his pillow.

My pillow. Where there definitely wasn't a gun before.

He blinks, lowers the gun. Says nothing.

"Jesus, Armando," I let out on a shaky breath. When he still doesn't speak, I say, "Listen, I have to go to the shop. It's cool for you to stay here and slee—"

But he's already up, swinging his legs over the side of the bed and sending Shadow leaping to the floor and arching his little back.

"You don't have to come. I think we've established now that I'm not going to talk, right? So I just need my phone, and I'll get out of here. You're welcome to stay."

Armando ignores me, pulling on a t-shirt he produces from a duffel bag under my bed.

Okay. So I guess he's moving in.

It shouldn't make me happy, but it sort of does.

He dresses in seconds, strapping the gun to his leg before he pulls his pants on. He produces my purse and phone and the keys to the van—this time from the oven. He still hasn't said a word when we walk out my front door.

When we get down to the sidewalk, Armando lifts his chin in the direction of the Starbucks on the corner. "You eat?" His voice is gruff and gravelly from sleep. Grumpy, even.

I don't know why I find it sexy.

"No." I'm sort of an erratic eater. I stress-eat at night but usually get too busy and behind for regular meals. Too bad missing meals hasn't resulted in a Hollywood figure. But screw Hollywood. I'm curvy in all the right places. A fact that Armando seems to enjoy with abandon.

He cuts into the Starbucks and pulls out his wallet. His eyes are dead this morning. I've seen them dead like this before, but there's a particular lights-out quality to them today. Or maybe it's the empath in me picking up on the complete lack of emotion on him.

I keep thinking about that gun he pointed at me this morning. The menace on his face before he saw it was me. I felt emotion from him then—it was deadly. Like a trapped animal about to kill for his freedom. What kind of life has he led that makes him wake up and point a gun first thing? What happened last night? I want to ask, but I know he won't answer.

Armando orders an egg sandwich and double espresso and turns to me. I order oatmeal and a latte. He pays again.

It's stupid—it's not that much money, but I like being out with Armando. Having him buy my meals and groceries. I like his take-chargeness. The way he didn't ask or discuss fixing the van with me, he just took it to a shop and got it done.

It might annoy some women, but I find it hot.

There's a sexy daddy element to him, and though I never knew that kink to be my jam, I'm starting to realize it is.

We take the food to go, and Armando drives again. I appreciate that, too. I don't care if it's my van, I hate driving in the city. I like someone else being in charge. I can simply eat my oatmeal, sip my latte, and stare out the window without a care in the world—if only momentarily.

He's still completely non-communicative, and I don't attempt conversation. I know lots of people who don't like to talk in the morning, even if they did get adequate sleep and weren't dealing with some kind of crisis all night. I'll wait until he warms up again.

At my shop, we enter through the back door. Armando stalks through the place and opens the blinds on the front windows. Then turns around my open sign with the hours.

"What the fuck, Hannah?" he snarls.

I freeze. The menace is back—I sense it all the way across the room and it scares me. "What?"

He points at the sign. "You're not supposed to be open on Sundays. What in the hell are you trying to pull?" He turns sideways, looking up and down the sidewalk through the front window.

Christ. Does he think I set him up? Like the cops are going to show up and bust him now? Or whoever's trying to kill him?

Chapter Thirty

Hannah

I march over to him, partly to conquer my own visceral fear of him in this state and partly because I'm pissed that he doesn't trust me. And pissed he scared me. "In case you didn't notice, Armando, I can't pay my rent. I have to stay open every minute I can, and that means working Sundays, too. I work *every* day. *Every* hour. It's the only way I can survive."

He blinks at me, some of the hardness in his expression falling away.

I stare back. "Don't yell at me like that again. You're scary when you're mean."

I expect him to be sorry. I want him to call me *baby girl*, pet my hair, hold me close, and promise to never be scary again, but instead he scowls. "Yeah, you should be scared of me, Flowers."

Offense cuts swift and deep, straight through my chest. I thrust my chin up. "That right? Well why don't you just say it then? Say whatever it is we're not coming back from.

Make your threats and be done with it. Then you can leave. It would be a whole lot easier for both of us."

He stands there a minute, conflict dancing over his face. I swear the room spins around us, like in those movies. And then his hand snaps out and captures the back of my head. His lips crash over mine. It's a juicy, lusty kiss because I give it right back.

This is what we do best. Our relationship may be a sham, communication is a joke, but we know this dance. I assume that's why he went for it. Just like I kissed him that first time when he was wondering what to do with me.

Do this.

This is what we do.

He breaks the kiss but doesn't release my head. "Is that what you want, Hannah? You want me to go?" Misery seeps out of him. A hint of desperation. He's holding my gaze like my answer will make the moon orbit.

"No," I admit. That's the last thing I want.

He pulls my mouth to his again and consumes me in a searing kiss. I kiss him back, my lips opening and closing against his, tugging on his.

"I'm sorry," he croaks when our lips part. "Someone shot up my place last night, and I'm paranoid as shit right now. I shouldn't have yelled. Especially at you."

My eyes round even though I suspected it was something awful like that.

"I *don't* want you scared." He shifts the hand behind my head to cradle the side of my face and runs his thumb across my lower lip. "I want these kisses like it's the end of the world. Fucking you like our lives depend on it."

A wave of heat crashes through me.

"You're the only thing keeping me sane right now. I'm

on the verge of losing my fucking mind. But it's you holding the key to my sanity, Hannah. You."

I freaking love the way he rasps my name. I initiate the kiss this time, pressing my breasts against his hard muscles. "Like our lives depend on it, huh?" I murmur when I come up for air.

He pushes me back against glass doors and closes the shades again. His hands are everywhere, stroking down my sides, squeezing my ass. I lift one leg to wrap around his waist, and when he shifts to put his forearm under my butt, the other one wraps too. He presses me against the window, knocking the blinds to thrust the bulge of his cock between my legs.

He dances his lips across my collarbone, and then stops to find my ear with his teeth, catching me with a shorter, sharper nip than before. I feel it all the way to my core. His voice is low and throaty, his words sending a sexy vibration through my ear. "You're so fucking gorgeous. And kissable. And fuckable. I want to bend you over right here, right now. I want to shove you up against this window and fuck you until you scream."

I'm too breathless to answer. I can't think of anything to say. "Do it, now, I need you."

His hand moves from my ass to my hip, and then around to my stomach, his fingertips pressing hard into my skin. "I want to watch you come from behind. I want to watch your sweet little pussy take my cock. I want to fuck you for hours."

"I want it," I tell him, my throat feeling tight and dry. I want it, but I don't want it to end. I want to stay here. I want to stay in this moment forever.

He kisses me again, and it's not gentle this time but urgent, and then he spins and carries me behind the counter to my desk. My ass touches down on the surface. The cool-ness shocking me back to reality.

Reality.

We're in the shop. My business. Reality.

"Wait," I pant. "We can't keep doing this."

It's too much. He's too much. I'm definitely feeling way too much.

He stiffens. Pulls back. I register the loss of his touch like a shock of cold water. "Yeah."

I'm immediately sorry for putting on the brakes. I reach for him. "Wait."

He steps back between my legs and strokes his palm up my bare thigh. His fingers reach the hem of my short t-shirt dress and slip under. Our foreheads touch. "Talk to me, Hannah."

Talk to him. This is the moment where I show my true colors, and he runs. But maybe that's for the best. That's what I need.

"I just..." I draw in a fortifying breath. "I don't do casual sex. I feel too much, you know? And I get attached too quickly..."

Worst thing ever to say to a guy.

But it's the truth.

"Does this feel casual to you?" Armando's voice sounds scratchy.

"No," I admit.

He picks up a swath of my hair and winds it around his fist, staring at the bleached curls mixing with the dark ones. "It doesn't feel casual to me. It feels desperate and life-giving. Like a starving baby's first pull of milk."

Oh, God. My heart tumbles. I freaking love knowing I'm giving him something he can't find anywhere else. Maybe even changing him. It brings significance to our dance. To who I am and what my life means. I lift my lips for a kiss, but he pulls back a half an inch and leaves me hanging.

"But if you need a breath, I'll step back. I don't force women."

Swoon. "Don't forget..." I breathe, looking up at him from under my lashes. "I like to be forced."

His sharp intake of breath is everything.

So is the way he slowly captures my wrist and tugs me off the desk then turns me around and bends me over. He pins my arm behind my back and slaps my ass. "So you do." His voice has that froggy sound again. He slowly takes my other wrist and twists it behind my back as well. My face presses against the smooth surface of the desk, the scent of ink and paper mingles with his masculine scent. He tugs up the hem of my dress, pushing the fabric up over the mounds of my ass. Then he peels down my panties just enough to stroke a hand over my ass. "You sore from that spanking I gave you before?"

My pussy contracts at the mention of what he did to me. Or maybe it's clenching at what he's doing now. I shake my head.

"You took it like a good girl, didn't you?"

Oh God.

So hot.

He slaps one cheek, catching the underside and making it reverberate right in my core. He strokes his hand over the sting. "Yeah, keep pushing me, Flowers, because I'm always gonna want to spank this ass pink."

I waggle my ass back and forth to tempt him again, and he spanks me. Rubs away the sting. "You are the hottest woman I've ever been with. By far." He spanks me again.

I close my eyes, soaking in both the sensations and his

words. He doesn't usually talk much, so his verbal expression now is a balm to my frayed nerves.

"And I like how much you feel." He smacks a little harder. "I like you attached." Another slap. "Because the only time I feel anything is when I'm with you."

Tears sting my eyes. For once, it seems like the guy I'm falling for is on the same page as me. It's a freaking miracle.

"Oh, fuck," he growls, his mouth on my neck. "You like when Daddy punishes you?" He spanks my ass again, and I mewl as I press against his palm.

He lifts me a little, and the rough fabric of his pants scrapes over the heated and ready flesh of my ass. I shudder, my hips rising to meet his touch.

"Y-Yes. I want it. I want it... *Daddy*." The word feels so fucking right rolling off my tongue.

"What do you want, Flowers?" he growls, his lips traveling up my neck to kiss me. "Tell me what you want."

"I want you to fuck me," I whisper, panting. "I want you to fuck me here, with my ass in the air and your cock inside me."

His hand grinds against my clit, and I whimper, my brain floating in a hazy sea of pleasure that's so much more intense than anything I've ever felt.

He presses a finger inside me. I'm so wet that it slides in easily, and my knees almost buckle. He slides in a second one and starts to stroke in and out while the tip of his thumb grinds over my aching clit.

I press my face against the desk, and my muffled cries of need echo in the room. The cool wood is against my cheek and his lips are on my back, whispering filthy things that go straight to my head.

"I'm going to fuck you like this, baby," he growls in my ear. "I'm going to make you come so hard with my cock in your sweet little pussy. But first, there's something you're going to do for me."

He slides his fingers out of me, and I whimper at the empty feeling.

He pulls the desk chair up behind him and sinks into it, freeing his erection. I turn to face him and drop to my knees. His gaze turns intent. Tortured, even. I totally owe him oral after how many times he's given me intense pleasure. He's always in charge, and I'm... well, I've been his prisoner. A role I seem to love.

But I want him to order me to suck him off. I want him to guide my head with my hair, commanding every move. I want to suck his dick because he demands it.

As if reading my mind, he says, "Put those lips of yours around my cock."

I wrap my hand around the base of his cock and swirl my tongue around the head. His erection juts out, suddenly thickening and lengthening in my hand.

"Oh fuck." he mutters, nostrils flaring, breath coming in sharply.

He fists my hair and tugs my head back, so my eyes lock with his. Heat floods between my legs. I'm turned on by the power I have over him and how much he has over me. I'm excited by how much pleasure I'm going to give him.

I hold his gaze as I slowly tighten my lips around his head and sink them lower.

His groan sounds pained. "Aw, Hannah." His fingers tangle in my hair and ball into a fist. "You—" he chokes as he pulls my head forward to take him in again.

It's another show of sexual domination. If you'd asked me before if I'd like it, I would've said no fricking way, but I do. Even as I'm slightly offended by the seeming lack of gratitude, by having my mouth used like nothing more than a fuck-hole, my pussy runs with arousal, my tightened nipples tingle, and I swirl my tongue around the underside of his cock with enthusiasm.

"Good girl, Hannah," he chants. "That's so fucking good. You're such a good girl." It's the third time he's called me *good girl*. Again, low-key offensive but so hot. His fist is tighter in my hair, pulling me over his length faster. I suck hard and use my hand to milk him, doing my best to give him pleasure.

His hips roll, and his cock slaps against my tongue. I wrap my lips around him and draw him into my mouth, my cheeks so hollowed his strokes slide with a wet sound from my lips to his balls. He's breathing faster, and I feel his biceps tense. I know he's close. I want to make him come.

I want the saltiness in my mouth.

His cock hardens and twitches. He groans and thrusts deeper, and I take him as greedily as I can.

I flex my hand around his length and massage the underside of his head with my tongue. His hand tightens in my hair, and I take him even deeper into my mouth, using my hand to stroke his length the way I know he likes.

He's still so hard it's almost impossible to fit him entirely in my mouth, and my jaw aches as I try to suck him.

I'm swallowing him; sucking him down as fast as I can. Fighting the gag reflex, my eyes water as I feel his cock swelling to an impossible size. He's getting ready to come, and when he does, I want it to be in my mouth. I want to taste him. I want to feel him shooting his cum on my tongue. I want to swallow him.

I start to run my tongue up and down his shaft and he tenses.

"Oh," he gasps. "Shit." He pulls me off, panting as he stares down at me with glassy eyes. "I wanted that to go on forever, but I wasn't gonna last." He shoves his hand in his pocket and pulls out a condom. "Climb on, Flowers. I'll give you a ride." His voice is a deep, sexy rumble. His dirty talk is on point today.

I ditch the panties still tangled around my thighs and straddle his waist while he rolls on the rubber.

"Oh God." A shudder of pleasure runs through him when I lower onto his dick. "Hannah. You're a fucking goddess. The flower goddess. Is there one?"

I've never heard this many unnecessary words come out of him. Something freed his tongue, and I absolutely love it. He palms my ass and controls my movements, even though he's on bottom. I take him deep when he thrusts up to meet me at the same time he yanks me in.

He kneads my ass. "I fucking love this ass, Hannah. It's so hot." He's losing his breath, sounding winded. I love watching his control slip. "Fucking flower goddess. Or wood nymph. You're like that fairy on your shoulder... but so much more. You're *carnal*." His fingers dig into my flesh. I'm seconds away from orgasming.

So is he, judging from the intensity of his thrusts, his gritted teeth and the wild look in his eyes. He bounces me over him, my legs dangling around his hips, my hair falling over the right side of my face.

"You're beautiful, so beautiful." He peers through heavy lids. "Are you close?" He adjusts his hands to bring his thumb to my clit.

"Yes! I'm ready!" I gasp. I'm past ready because the moment he rubs my clit, I go off, my muscles spasming around his cock.

"Oh *fuck*," he roars, forgetting my clit to grab my hips and yank me up and down over his cock.

He comes, lifting us both into the air as he thrusts so

deep in me he leaves the chair. He puts the edge of my butt on the desk and pounds into me as he comes and comes.

I fall back on my elbows, panting, watching the guy who was made of stone this morning come unglued.

In the best possible way.

"*Cristo,*" he mutters when he opens his eyes and takes me in. He loops his arm behind my back and pulls me up against his chest. "Are you good?"

"Yes." I bite his chest and squeeze his cock with my core. I let out a breathy laugh. And then I'm suddenly crying.

Not sad tears—just a release. But I hate when I do this.

Armando's arm tightens around me. I expect him to freak out, thinking he hurt me or something. Or worse, to pull way back because I got too intense. That's what usually happens. This is usually where the guy freaks out and bails.

He doesn't say a word, though. Doesn't ask me what's wrong. Just holds me against his rock-solid chest and lets me cry into his shirt.

When it finally passes, he eases away and wipes my tears with his thumbs. "I fucking love your tears," he murmurs.

"What?"

He shakes his head. "Ugh, that sounded wrong. I didn't mean it like that."

I wait, but he doesn't elaborate. He's already distancing —doing the thing that always happens. But his words—those were different.

I catch his hand. "Say it again. What did you mean?"

He cradles the side of my face with his calloused palm. "You're okay, right? That was just... you? Or did I fuck up again?"

The *again* makes my stomach twist. In a good sort of way. Because he cares about screwing up with me.

I shake my head. "Yeah, just me being... too much. As usual." I say it in a defeated tone, not because he's made me feel defeated but from the accumulation of a lifetime of feeling everything too much.

He lowers his head to catch my eyes. "Nah. Not too much. I fucking loved it. You're like... some wild mythical creature—" he stops, looking up like he's searching for words. "I don't want to say *unicorn* because that's dumb. But something like that."

My heart spills over, coming out my mouth, filling my chest. A couple fresh tears come out of my eyes. Armando thumbs them away again.

"I don't know, Flowers. You're wide open. You take it all. You just fucking *receive* from me. And I think it's beautiful. And if I'm supposed to say *sorry* now, I will. But it would be a lie because I love seeing you crack apart and bleed your essence all over the place then gather it up and start over again."

I stare into Armando's hazel eyes, drinking up his praise. Expanding. Expanding into myself. Who I really am. The person I am with Armando—that's the real me. I'm more myself with him than anyone else. Possibly even including myself. He celebrates the parts of me I don't even like.

And knowing that, believing that he thinks I'm special, changes me. Makes me stronger. More whole.

He glances around the shop and smirks. "Something about the Garden of Eden. It makes me want to sin. Over and over." He kisses me. "And over again."

Chapter Thirty-One

Armando

Coming down from post-orgasmic euphoria, I decide it's time to discuss something that's been weighing heavy on me since I woke up.

I lean my forehead against Hannah's. "Am I bad for you? Do you want me to go? Honestly?"

She rolls her head against mine in a negative. "No," she whispers. "I never wanted you to go. This is what I was afraid of—what I was trying to avoid. But it's already here."

"It's already here," I repeat. I understand logically, but I have no idea what she feels. I'm empty, and she's too full. Maybe that's why we fit. What works for us.

There's no comprehending Hannah because she's so different from me and the people I've known. That's why she seems mythical. Her capacity for acceptance is monumental.

I stroke her unruly curls then scrunch them when I find them not so strokable. They were made for fisting, for sure. "So, am I forgiven? I'm sorry I was a dick."

She lets out a puff of air like a laugh. "We're good."

I ease out of her and dispose of the condom in the trash beside the desk. "What can I do around here to help?" I put my dick away and zip up my pants. Retrieve her panties from the floor and squat down to thread them over her ankles.

"Um..." She looks afraid to ask me something.

"Yeah? What? Name it, Flowers."

"Wanna help me clean out the cooler? That's what I usually do on Sundays before I open."

"I'll clean it. You do whatever else you need to do."

Her face lights with guilty surprise. She drops off the desk and pulls her panties up. "Really? It's kind of a shitty job although it will be easier for you because you're strong."

I scrunch up my forehead, trying to figure out what takes strength.

"You have to move all the heavy buckets of flowers around to mop up underneath. I usually end up slopping so much water around I get drenched. In the winter, I take my pants off before I go in, so they don't get soaked."

My dick sprouts a semi. "Making a note. Be here on Sundays in the winter."

Her smile is a sweet reward. Hell, I'd clean out a room full of dogshit for that smile.

I already know where her cleaning supplies are since I had to bleach the hell out of her floor. I pull them out and head into the cooler and move all the buckets of flowers to the hallway to sweep and mop.

I'm at it for a while before I realize something: I'm awake. Alive. That hollow-man deadness that settled in hard last night has dissipated. In fact, my whole body's buzzing. Not just that, but there's something there I haven't felt in years.

A thread of happiness.

I'm one week out of the pen with a gang trying to kill me, and I'm buzzing with a newfound contentment.

Hannah makes me happy. That's the only explanation for it. I like being around her. Things make more sense when she's around. And of course, the sex is off the charts good.

I hear a scream from the kitchenette, and all that happiness flips to furious purpose.

No one fucks with my girl.

Gun drawn and pointed, I'm there in a flash, readying to fucking kill whoever's in there. Ready to give up my life if it will save hers.

I whip around the corner and skid to a stop, pointing the gun right and left.

Um...

No one's in there with her. She's frozen in the middle of the tiny break room, her eyes wide and terrified.

Because of me. The gun.

I quickly lower it. "You screamed."

She lets out a shaky laugh and points toward the floor in the corner. "There's a mouse."

"A mouse." I will my heartbeat to slow. Try to take the death grip off the pistol. I flip it to the side and cock my head. "Want me to shoot it?" I deadpan.

She smiles at me and walks forward until her soft breasts press against my ribs. "A joke. I think that was your first."

Was it?

Damn.

I *am* coming back to life.

"You looked really scary when you came in here." She purrs it like it turned her on.

I shove the pistol in the back of my waistband and loop an arm around her. "I wondered."

"What?"

"What made you kiss me that first time? You like the tough guy?"

"I like *you*," she confesses, her hands sliding up my pecs. "I always did."

"Yeah?" That surprises me. I remember her from before, but she was young. And off-limits. Plus, I was engaged. I thought she was cute but didn't pay much more attention. Now I marvel at how much I missed. I wanna go back in time and review all my visits to the shop to put her in full focus.

"And, yes, I like that you're dangerous. It's a total turn-on."

"You're something, Flowers." I stroke her cheek with my thumb.

She backs up. "So can you be dangerous to my mice?"

I chuckle. "Yeah, sure. You got traps?"

"Um, yes. I bought some, but I couldn't bring myself to use them because I can't face cleaning up dead mice. Same reason I haven't used poison."

My lips twitch. Holy shit. I may actually smile. Didn't know my mouth remembered how. "So you're just putting up with the mice instead."

She nods. "Exactly."

"I'll take care of it for you, doll. I'm your guy. You won't have to worry about them again."

And as I go back to cleaning out the cooler, I notice it again: that lightness around me suddenly.

Like there's a reason to go on living.

I dare say I'm starting to feel normal again. If that's even possible.

"Hey, Flowers!" I call out from the cooler, feeling it's time to face something else I've been avoiding since getting out of prison. I thought it would be a long time until I'd be in the mood again for it, but I'm suddenly feeling now's as good a time as any.

She opens up the cooler and leans against the frame. "You rang?" Her smile is so damn big on her face. I could stare at it all day.

"It's Sunday."

She nods. "We've established that already."

"Take the day off."

"I can't. I told you—"

I reach into my wallet, pull out a hundred-dollar bill, and place it into her hand. "Take this as paid time off and come with me to church."

I need to expunge my sins. To make myself clean to be worthy of this treasure of a woman. I don't know if that shit is real, but my ma believes in it. She lights a candle for me every time she goes to mass—twice a week.

It may not be real, but it seems like a nod in that direction is warranted. For Hannah.

Her eyes widen. "Church?"

"It's Sunday. Church."

"Now?"

I nod. "Mass is already over, but the doors will be open."

She looks down at her clothing. "I need to go home and change."

I take her by the hand and lead her away from the cooler. "Trust me. After the secrets and confessions this church has heard, the last thing we'll be judged over is our clothing. Besides," I press my lips to her forehead, "you're beautiful."

"I didn't figure you for a church man."

"I used to be," I confess. "It's been a long time. But it's long overdue. Plus, I promised Father Fantoni I'd come by, and I haven't yet. I may be a sinner, but I'm a man of my word."

She gives me a soft smile. "Okay, let me go make sure we're locked in the front." She hurries to the front door and freezes with a gasp. I instantly reach for my gun but then realize it's probably just another mouse.

"Armando," she whispers, fear lacing her voice.

Pulling my gun, I rush towards her.

She points through a crack of the blinds and the door. "There's a man outside."

I release the safety, ready to defend the woman I— I see *Marco* on the other side.

Releasing the breath I'd been holding, putting away the gun, opening the door, and punching my cousin playfully in the arm, I say, "I could have shot you right there, man."

"Leo and I told you we'd have extra eyes stationed." Marco scans Hannah from head to toe, and I see approval in the devilish smile he offers.

"Why you? Not one of your men?"

Marco shrugs. "It's Sunday. Most of the men are with their families today. I have nothing better to do. Besides, if you want something done right, do it yourself."

Hannah clears her throat behind me, reminding me of my manners. "Marco, this is Hannah. Hannah, this is my cousin Marco."

She extends her hand, and with the sweetest voice says, "Nice to meet you, officially. I remember your face from you shopping on occasion in the store."

"You're the owner now, right?" Marco asks.

"Yes."

"We were just leaving. Going to St. Andrews. Care to come?" I ask him.

Marco chuckles. "If I step foot in that church, I'll be struck down. It's been so long since I've confessed that I wouldn't even know where to begin."

"Perfect," I say. "Then we can be struck down together."

Marco's eyes dart back to Hannah then to me. "Church, huh?"

"It's Sunday," I state.

"Yeah, I know what day it is." Marco smiles. "Well then, church it is." He directs his next comment to Hannah. "But I'm warning you, Hannah. Don't stand too close to us. It may not be a pretty sight if we burst into flames."

Chapter Thirty-Two

H*annah*

"Good girls get ice cream after church," Armando says as he leads me down the street hand in hand.

We just said our goodbyes to Marco. It took Armando practically threatening the man to leave us alone for a few hours. Armando promised that we'd head back to my apartment and stay put, so I'm confused as to why we aren't heading home.

"Growing up, my mother used to always reward me with ice cream if I was good during church service," he adds. He looks down at me and winks. "You were good."

My body lights up, feeling warm and fuzzy. We're holding hands like a couple, walking under the sunlight to go get ice cream. It's like we're on an official date. We're spending a leisurely Sunday together. Everything feels so normal and so right.

The ice cream shop is only a block away, and the minute I see it, I'm in love with the charm. The little shop is painted a pastel pink and white, with a giant ice cream cone sign hanging over the entrance. The air inside is cool and sweet, and I can hear the gentle chime of the bell above the door as we walk in.

The quaint space has a vintage feel to it, and the aroma of freshly made waffle cones hits us the moment we enter. The place is bustling with people, but we manage to find a free table in the corner. The sound of a guitar being played fills the air, and I notice a young man sitting in the corner, strumming away on his instrument.

"What's your favorite flavor?" he asks.

"Whatever you have," I answer. When it comes to ice cream, there is no such thing as a bad flavor.

Armando goes to order, leaving me to enjoy the music. As he waits in line, he turns around and waves at me, a grin spreading across his face. My heart flutters as I wave back, feeling a warm sensation in my chest. When he returns to the table, he has two cones in his hand.

"Two scoops. One is caramel chocolate, and the other is cookie dough." I see pride on his face that he's picked the best two flavors there are.

"Perfect."

We sit there, enjoying our ice cream and listening to the music. It's simple. Relaxed.

"You grow up in Chicago?" Armando asks, studying me over the top of his ice cream cone.

"Yep. Born and raised."

"Do your parents live here?"

I nod. "Yes. My mom's a nurse, and my dad works in construction."

It's crazy to have this casual conversation with Armando. Nothing about Armando and me up to this point has been simply casual. It's like we're the only two people in the world right now, and nothing else matters.

"You?"

He nods. "Born and bred. It was just my ma and me, but we're Italian, so I have a huge extended family. Twenty-some cousins. I'm closest with Marco and his brother Leo. They're like brothers to me, really. Oh, how we used to hell around." A warmth comes into his normally dead gaze. The light in his eyes makes me feel more alive than I've felt in a long time. He's actually sharing. He's opening up when I wasn't sure that was a possibility with this man.

"Thanks for this," I say when we finish our treat. "I haven't had a real day off in a long time," I admit. "And even when I tried, my mind was always so full of worry. So this is a rare day for me."

"We're going to have to fix that."

"*We?*"

He smirks. "You're stuck with me, Flowers." His face grows serious, his eyes darken. "You work too hard. You take on too much on those perfect shoulders of yours. It's time you have someone help with the heavy lifting."

I've always been an independent woman. Someone who wants to stand on my own two feet, but damn if it doesn't feel good to have a man sitting across from me... protecting and looking out for my well-being.

I finish my cone and wipe my mouth with a napkin. "Thank you," I say, not wanting the moment to end.

"Of course," he replies, taking my hand in his again. "We should do this more often."

I nod, feeling a smile spread across my face. "I'd like that."

As we leave the shop, I realize that this is the happiest I've been in a long time. I don't know what the future holds, but I know that I want him by my side. I want to hold his hand and walk under the sunlight every day. I want to listen to him talk and figure out how to make him laugh, but I also don't mind his darkness and the shadows that haunt his eyes.

I want to taste more ice cream with him and explore more charming little shops, but I also want to be there for him when the scars of his past come back or his demons conquer the day. I want to fall in love with him, and I want him to fall in love with me.

We stroll down the street, enjoying the warm breeze and each other's company. It doesn't seem like we have a destination in mind, but that doesn't matter. We're content just being together.

Suddenly, he stops in front of a small boutique. It's filled with vintage clothes and accessories. He turns to me, his eyes shining with excitement. "Let's go in."

I follow him inside, feeling like a kid in a candy store. The boutique is even more charming than the ice cream shop. The walls are covered in bright wallpaper, and the clothes on the racks are like nothing I've ever seen before. It's like stepping back in time, but also so trendy.

He starts picking out clothes for me to try on, and I can't help but laugh. He has a great sense of style, and everything he chooses would look amazing on me. As we browse through the racks, I feel a sense of closeness with him that I've never felt before. It's like we're in our own little world, and nothing can bring us down.

After trying on a few outfits due to his urging, I settle on a vintage floral dress. He pays for it without hesitation, insisting that I look beautiful in it. I'm noticing that he likes to take care of me, and I need to allow him to do it. I need to resist the urge to fight him on money and to constantly worry over every little cent.

As we leave the shop, he says, "I suppose we should

head home. If Marco or one of his men get there to stand guard before we arrive, my cousin is going to kill me."

"We wouldn't want that," I say with a smile.

"You haven't seen Marco mad," he says with the hint of a smile.

Happiness on Armando is a good look. He's so fucking hot right now.

I lean forward, so close I can feel his warm breath on his face and smell the sugary sweetness from the ice cream.

"Kiss me," I say. "Kiss me like a boyfriend kisses a girlfriend."

He looks at me with a mix of surprise and hesitation, as if trying to read my mind. I sense his heart racing, and I know that I am pushing him way beyond his comfort zone. I said *boyfriend* and *girlfriend*. But I don't care. I want him to kiss me, to claim me as his own, to make me forget about everything else in the world.

He leans in slowly, his lips hovering just inches from mine. His hand drops to my waist, pulling me closer to him. I close my eyes and take a deep breath, trying to calm my racing heart. And then, finally, his lips meet mine in a tender, almost hesitant kiss.

At first, it's gentle and tentative, as if he's afraid of hurting me. But then, as I respond eagerly, he deepens the kiss, his tongue probing my lips. I moan softly, my hands clutching his shoulders, urging him on. He presses me against the wall of the boutique, his body hard against mine, and I feel a surge of desire like nothing I have ever felt before.

I wrap my arms around his neck, my fingers tangling in the short hair at the nape of his neck. I feel the strength in his arms as he holds me close. With a groan, he breaks the kiss, pulling back to look at me. "What are we doing?" His voice is husky.

"We're kissing," I say, a smile playing at the corners of my lips.

"Like boyfriend and girlfriend?"

"Exactly," I say simply, before pulling him in for another kiss. This time, he responds with even more passion, his hands roaming over my body as he kisses me deeply.

As our mouths move in perfect harmony, I realize that this is what I've been missing. Passion, desire, and the thrill of the unknown. I don't know where this will lead, but for now, all that matters is the heat between us, the hunger in our kiss and the promise of more to come.

Chapter Thirty-Three

Armando

We enter her tiny apartment, kissing, surrounded in a hurricane of lust and desire. I need this woman more than I need to breathe.

As we stumble through the door, our lips pressed together in a frenzied passion, a sense of relief washes over me. Finally, I'm here, with her, and nothing else in the world matters. Her apartment is small, cramped even, but I don't care. All I need is her. We're two animals returning to our den. Our den of sins.

My hands roam over her body, tracing the curves and dips of her figure. Heat radiates off her skin, and it only fuels my desire further. I need to be inside her. Now.

I lift her off the ground, her legs wrapping around my waist as we stumble towards the bed. Her scent fills my nostrils, intoxicating me further.

As we collapse onto the bed, I break our kiss for just a moment to look into her eyes. They're dark, filled with a hunger that matches my own. I need her, all of her, and I know she needs the same from me.

"I'm going to fuck you like a boyfriend fucks a girl-friend," I say, remembering her request earlier and how she wanted me to kiss her.

Her hands are in my hair, pulling me closer. I feel her urgency, her need for me. "No. Fuck me like an animal would fuck his prey."

This girl... she's fucking everything. Everything.

I dip my head down to kiss her again, my tongue slipping into her mouth as she moans in pleasure. Our bodies are pressed together, my hardening cock aching to be inside her. Sliding my hand down between her legs, I stroke into her wetness and know that she's ready for me, and it only spurs me on further. I need to be inside her. I need to make her mine.

With one hand, I undo the buttons of her blouse, revealing the soft skin underneath. My lips leave hers, trailing down her neck and chest, leaving a trail of kisses in their wake. My other hand reaches for her skirt, pulling it down her body until it falls to the floor.

My hands roam everywhere, seeking out every inch of her skin. She moans and writhes beneath me, her own fingers gripping my hair and pulling me closer as if scared I'll leave her alone.

My mouth finds her nipple, and I begin to suck on it, teasing it with my tongue while the other hand finds and begins to tease the other one.

Her body trembles beneath mine, her breathing growing ragged. I slide my hand down her body, my fingers desperate to find her wetness.

She lifts her legs and wraps them around my waist, pulling me closer to her, desperate for me to enter her. When my fingers find the edge of her panties, I hook a finger in the side and pull them down with ease.

I slide one finger inside her, taking it out and sliding it back in again as she moans in pleasure. I tease her, torturing her with my touch. I want her to beg for me. I want her to know my power over her.

"Please," she breathes out. "Please, I need you. Fuck me."

My fingers are moving faster now, sliding in and out of her, my thumb rubbing her clit in quick little circles.

She throws her head back and moans, her voice filled with desire.

It's the most erotic sound I've ever heard. All I want is to have her screaming beneath me, moaning my name for the rest of my life.

She claws at my clothes, desperately ridding me of them and tossing them to the floor.

I need to be inside her, now.

With a quickness, I undo my pants, sliding them off and tossing them to the floor. I tear off my boxers as she reaches down to wrap her hand around my cock. I moan in pleasure, knowing what's coming next.

My cock throbs, precum oozing from the tip as it waits to be inside her. Her fingers slide up and down my shaft, teasing the head with her thumb. I groan as she plays with me, my body tense as I wait for what's to come.

I slide two fingers into her welcoming channel. She twitches and tenses with the slightest touch, like she's already close to climaxing.

I need to be inside her, now.

The tip of my cock finds her wet entrance, and she thrusts her hips up, desperate to take me inside her. She is dripping wet, and it makes my cock slip in effortlessly, the heat of her folds embracing my cock, taking me inside her.

Her body shudders as I enter her, and I can tell she's desperate for me to move.

I pull out my cock until just the tip is inside her, before plunging back in. My hands grip her hips as I take her in pure animalistic bliss. I'm not being gentle, and with each aggressive push, she meets me with just as much force. She arches her back, meeting each thrust with her own. The look of pure pleasure on her face is indescribable. I'm taking her, and she loves every second of it.

I pull out, and she whimpers. I want her to need me.

"Beg for me," I growl. "Beg for me to fuck you."

"Please," she replies. "I need you. Please, fuck me."

Her voice is desperate, and I need to hear more.

I slide deep inside her, her legs wrapping around me, pulling me closer to her. "Fuck me," she says. "Fuck me like an animal."

I pull out, but she's ready for me. She's desperate for me, and I know she wants to be filled with me.

"Please, baby. Fill me. Let me come. Make me come," she cries out. "I need it. I need you. Fuck me. Please."

It's the most beautiful sound I've ever heard. I plunge my cock into her again and again, my pace quickening with each thrust, each movement.

As we move together, we're moaning, panting, and whispering. I sense her getting closer, her body tensing beneath mine. Her fingernails dig into my back as she tries to hold on.

My cock throbs as she thrusts her hips up, meeting each thrust with a moan of pleasure. The pleasure grows so great that I feel my own orgasm building.

It's the most intense feeling I've ever had. My cock throbs and pulses as I plunge in and out of her. She whimpers, begging me to make her come over and over again.

She's getting closer now. I can tell as her moans grow louder, and her body begins to writhe beneath mine.

"Come with me," I growl. "Come now."

I plunge my cock deep inside her, filling her and pushing her over the edge as she shudders beneath me. Her pussy clenches my cock, her juices flowing out of her as she screams.

Her body shakes, and she bucks her hips against mine, her orgasm shaking her to the core. My balls pump once, twice, four times as I bury myself deep inside her, releasing my seed into her.

I don't know how long we lay there, sticky, hot, and complete. Our breaths feel as if they morph to one, our heartbeat finds the same cadence. And for the first time in my entire life, I feel like I'm home.

Chapter Thirty-Four

Hannah

"So he's living with you now?" Josie asks. "Don't you think things are moving a little fast?"

I shrug. "In a way, yes. I don't know. It's not the normal situation between us. The way we hooked up sort of amplified things."

"Is he the reason there's a goon following me to and from work now?"

"He's making sure we're safe," I defend. "It's just while things settle with a situation with his work."

"Are we in danger?" Her eyes widen. "I didn't sign on for this shit."

"He's just being overly protective. It comes with the territory of what he does."

"Is this all worth it? Is he good?" Josie asks in a teasing voice as she pulls a tired bouquet out of the cooler and dumps the water in my industrial sink.

I have the usual anxious feeling in the pit of my stomach that I always have when she's working, but even so, I'm relieved to hash through the details of Armando with her.

My eyelids flutter. "So good. Like three times yesterday and once this morning good."

"Oh damn. That's so hot. So is it like... an arrangement? Like you pimped yourself out for the rent? Or what?"

I hurl a dead rose at her head. "Bitch, I did not whore myself out. He just offered to pay the rent. And I accepted the offer."

"Mmm hmm. And how did that go down, exactly?"

Okay, crap. I can't tell her the real story. "All right, yeah, I pimped myself out," I mumble, like I'm coming clean.

Josie's eyes pop. "Oh, that's hot. I think that's so hot. And he just ponied up the money and said *get in my bed, bitch?*"

I snort-laugh. "Yeah, just like that."

Josie eyes me with unveiled curiosity. She's as tall as I am short—six foot one, and the shortest of all her siblings. And yes, they all played basketball. Her family immigrated from Brazil when she was four. Dark-skinned like me, she's beautiful, with bleached-blonde hair blooming in a halo around her head. She's the reason I bleached the ends of my curls although I didn't go quite as light as she did.

She cocks her head. "I can't decide what I think about all this."

"What do you mean?" I may sound slightly defensive.

"I don't know. You look happy. Happier than you have in a while. But this is so out of character for you, I feel like I might need to call an intervention or something."

My face grows warm. "I like him, Jos."

She points a stern finger at me. "Don't tell him that. And do not cry! Please tell me you haven't already cried."

I cringe a little. Josie knows how relationships always end for me. We've been friends since high school—and there's definitely a pattern. I get attached too quickly—

assign too much meaning to things. Then I blurt, "I love you!" or some other such clingy thing. Or I burst into tears or somehow over-emote about something, and then it's over. The guy hightails it away from me. I'm way too much for him.

"Well, I did cry," I admit. "—It was after sex, though!" I add quickly when Josie shoots me the *It's all over* look.

"Uh huh. And how did that go?"

"Um." I consider. "Actually not horrible. He rolled with it. Like he didn't seem to think it was that big a deal." Now that I'm saying it, I'm surprised. Why didn't he get uncomfortable or try to fix it or think I was nuts? "I don't know... maybe women routinely cry after sex with him," I joke, but thinking of him having sex with other women makes the words turn sour in my mouth. "He is that good."

Josie puts her hands on her hips. "When was this?"

The cringey feeling returns. "Yesterday... maybe the day before that too." And this morning, he abruptly ended our joined-at-the-hip thing.

He left while I was still asleep in bed. Just kissed my forehead and said he had to go to work. Like it was no big deal, and I hadn't just been his prisoner for days. He told me a man would be outside the shop all day, and to not leave without someone with me. But he wasn't sitting on me anymore. He told me he'd check in later as a normal couple would do.

I'd been thinking it meant he finally trusted me, but maybe it was the crying. Or me. Being too much, as always. He was bailing.

The bells on the door jingle and Jack, the FedEx guy comes in. "Package for you, young lady." He beams at me in a fatherly way as he hands over a padded envelope. "You have to sign for this one."

Perplexed, I sign his electronic clipboard and examine the package. I haven't ordered anything since I don't have any credit left on my credit card or cash in my bank account —unless I count the money Armando put there.

I tear open the packaging to find a tiny jewelry box. "Oh wow." My pulse quickens. He bought me a gift.

A gift.

That means something, doesn't it?

Josie makes an excited humming sound. "Somebody likes you."

"Oh wow," I murmur again, prying open the small lid with trembling fingers. "Wow." It seems to be the only word I remember how to say. I crack open the box. Inside is a gold nose ring with a diamond on the end.

Josie snatches up the certificate that came with it. "Eighteen carat gold with a conflict-free VVS diamond." She looks up at me. "*Dayum.* He definitely likes you."

I can't stop the stupid smile that plasters my face.

He likes me.

It's a thoughtful gift. It fits me. It's not some stupid diamond heart necklace or other cliché jewelry. He bought something that I'd like and wear. I slip out my plain gold ring and put in the diamond. "How's it look?"

Josie grins. "It's perfect."

"Yeah, it is." Of course he would've ordered this a couple days ago if it arrived today, so it's no guarantee he's still into me, but I suddenly feel much more hopeful that we have a chance.

I definitely want us to have a chance.

But I shouldn't start assigning meaning to things. This is how every relationship goes wrong for me.

I look over at Josie, thinking this would be a good time to

talk to her about how her working here could use some adjustment. Now, while we're comfortable and close.

"Listen, Josie..."

"Hm?"

"Um, I was wondering... how do you like working here?"

She peers at me, a touch of alarm on her face. Butterflies flap their wings wildly in my belly. Up my esophagus. Into my throat.

"I like it, why?" Is it me, or does she sound nervous?

"Oh, um, I..." Christ! I'm a stammering fool! "Good. I'm glad. Just checking." I turn and flee to the workshop.

Great. That went well. Gah. I'm so not cut out to run this business on my own!

I need a breath of fresh air and step outside into the alley. I see Marco leaning against the wall, scrolling through his phone.

"Hey, Marco," I say, feeling both odd and protected that he is here. "Armando told me one of your men would be here today. I wasn't expecting you."

"I don't mind." He glances up from his phone and smiles. Marco looks a lot like Armando—the bloodline visibly thick between the two. So much so that I'm missing him already and hoping he'll call me soon. "I like feeling out the situation first."

"Oh yeah?" I lift an eyebrow and ask, "What do you *feel* about the situation?"

"My cousin likes you. A lot."

My heart flutters, and my breath hitches. "He does?"

"He does." Marco tilts his head and seems to scrutinize every inch of my face. "He's never taken anyone to church before."

I didn't know that, but I like hearing it.

"I'm assuming the feeling is mutual?" he asks.

My face feels as if it's a hundred degrees. My palms are sweaty, and I suddenly wish I had a cigarette. I don't smoke, but at least I'd have something to do, so I wouldn't feel so awkward simply standing in the alley with a man I barely knew.

"It's mutual."

"And do you know what that means?"

I look up and lock eyes with him.

"You understand the life Armando leads, right?"

I nod and focus my stare on my worn Converse. "I do."

"It can't be changed."

"I have no desire to change him."

Marco takes a step toward me and uses his finger to tilt my chin up, so I have to look into his eyes. He opens his mouth to talk, but my phone rings, interrupting us.

"It could be Armando," I say, not recognizing the number, but hoping it's him.

Marco nods to the phone for me to answer it.

Chapter Thirty-Five

*A*rmando

"Give Nonna a kiss for me, okay?"

My mom calls me on her way to the airport. I bought her a ticket to see my nonna in Arizona for a couple weeks, just so I didn't have to worry about anyone fucking with her.

"I will. I know there's some kind of trouble, and I know you can't tell me, but Mando?"

I suck in my breath. "Yeah, ma?"

"You take care of yourself." Her voice wobbles.

"I will, ma. I am. I just need to know you're safe."

"Are you staying at your apartment? Maybe that's not a good idea."

"I'm not. I'm lying low. Actually..."

I don't know why I have the urge to tell her. Only because she deserves something—anything—to brighten her thoughts about me.

"I met a girl. I'm crashing at her place until things cool off."

My mom makes a little sound of surprise. "That's great. You must like her if you're telling me about her."

"Yeah. I do."

"Does she make you happy?"

"She does. I didn't think it was possible. But she does."

"You deserve to be happy."

"I'm not sure what I deserve," I admit.

"You may have made mistakes, son. You may make many more to come. But the one thing I know is you deserve happiness. Don't resist it."

"I'm trying not to."

"What's her name?"

I hesitate because we're on the phone, but I doubt the guys looking for me are sophisticated enough to pull off some kind of tap. Besides, it's a burner I picked up on the day I got out of prison.

"Hannah."

"Hannah. Is she Catholic?"

Leave it to my ma to ask that question. "We went to church together yesterday."

"That's great. Did you confess?"

"I did."

It was the hardest and yet easiest thing I'd done in a long time. I did it for me. I did it for Hannah, and I did it to try to free my soul. I spoke the words I needed to and didn't hold back:

Bless me father for I have sinned.

My soul is damaged beyond repair.

It's been five years since my last confession.

Five years since my mother wept as they led me out of court in handcuffs.

Three years since I killed a man in prison. Now there's a price on my head.

Three days out, and I commit another sin to stay alive.

And then another with her, my beautiful witness.

And another with her.

And another.

I'm not asking for absolution.

All I really want is her.

"That makes me happy to hear," she says. "I'd like to meet her."

Something crowds my chest. Because I don't get to do normal. I probably won't get to introduce Hannah to my mom even though I'm sure they'd love each other. They're both warm, open-hearted women.

"Yeah, we'll see. Travel safe, ma."

"I will. Be careful, Mando. I'll be praying for you."

"I know you will. I love you." I say the words, but I think I might also have a glimmer of the feeling, too. Or just the memory of the feeling. Moms are powerful that way.

I end the call as I head to my new job. The don told me to call in sick but fuck it—I'm going. Fuck the Hermanos. They can come for me on the construction site if they want. I have a piece, and I'm ready for them.

I need to get a life going on the outside. Hiding at Hannah's forever is not an option, as much as I enjoy her. Yeah, *enjoy*.

That's a word I didn't think I'd be using any time soon.

I was balls deep in her again multiple times last night. One epic session involved me putting her on her knees on the bed and fucking her with my thumb in her ass. Then, before the sun even rose, I found my hand cupping her pussy when I woke, and it was on again. I rolled her to her belly and spread her legs wide. Held her down with my hand at her nape because she likes a little struggle.

She came twice—she's so damn responsive. So brave.

I realized that at some point last night. The level of vulnerability she displays can only be born from immense courage. Her example is the only thing showing me the way back to being human again.

Not that I think there can be many humans like her.

It's so funny to me how normal she seems—like an ordinary twenty-something-year-old. She'd fit in anywhere. But she's anything but.

I can't get her out of my mind. I can't get the smell of her out of my nose. I can't make the vision of her lying in bed staring up at me to go away. She's everywhere I look. She's consuming.

Before I get out of the van of hers I'm borrowing, I decide I need to give her a call. I know Marco is standing guard, but it will put my mind at ease to hear her voice.

"Hello, Flowers," I say when she answers the phone.

"I was hoping it was you." I hear the smile in her voice.

"How has the morning been so far?"

"Good. Josie arrived on time, and we've been talking."

"Did Marco arrive? He said he would."

"Yes, in fact, I'm standing outside right now talking to him."

Just as I'm getting ready to tell her to get back inside where it's safe, I hear the worst noise imaginable. It's a loud *pop, pop, pop*, followed by an ear-piercing scream.

"Hannah!"

The scream doesn't stop.

"Hannah!"

And then there is silence...

* * *

Thank you for reading *Den of Sins*! *Rooted in Sin, the conclusion to Hannah and Armando's story is available for order here.* If you enjoyed this book, please consider leaving a review—they make a huge difference for indie authors.

Want Another FREE Renee Rose book?

Read Her Royal Master for free here: https://hyzr.app.link/herroyalmaster

Want Another FREE Renee Rose book?

Also by Alta Hensley

Gods Among Men Series:

Villains Are Made

Monsters Are Hidden

Vipers Are Forbidden

* * *

Secret Bride Trilogy:

Captive Bride

Kept Bride

Taken Bride

* * *

Wonderland Trilogy:

King of Spades

Queen of Hearts

Ace of Diamonds

* * *

Dark Pen Series:

Devil's Contract

Dirty Ledger

Dangerous Notes

* * *

<u>Spiked Roses Billionaires' Club:</u>

Bastards & Whiskey

Villains & Vodka

Scoundrels & Scotch

Devils & Rye

Beasts & Bourbon

Sinners & Gin

* * *

<u>Evil Lies Series:</u>

The Truth About Cinder

The Truth About Alice

* * *

<u>Breaking Belles Series:</u>

Elegant Sins

Beautiful Lies

Opulent Obsession

Inherited Malice

Delicate Revenge

Lavish Corruption

* * *

Gold In Locks

Sick Crush

Secret Bride

Captive Vow

Ruin Me

Delicate Scars

Other Titles by Renee Rose

Hero

Rebel

Warrior

Vegas Underground Mafia Romance

King of Diamonds

Mafia Daddy

Jack of Spades

Ace of Hearts

Joker's Wild

His Queen of Clubs

Dead Man's Hand

Wild Card

Contemporary

Daddy Rules Series

Fire Daddy

Hollywood Daddy

Stepbrother Daddy

Master Me Series

Her Royal Master

Her Russian Master

Her Marine Master

Yes, Doctor

Double Doms Series

Feral

Savage

Fierce

Ruthless

Wolf Ridge High Series

Alpha Bully

Alpha Knight

Step Alpha

Bad Boy Alphas Series

Alpha's Temptation

Alpha's Danger

Alpha's Prize

Alpha's Challenge

Alpha's Obsession

Alpha's Desire

Alpha's War

Alpha's Mission

Alpha's Bane

Alpha's Secret

Alpha's Prey

Alpha's Sun

Shifter Ops

Alpha's Moon

Alpha's Vow

About Alta Hensley

Alta Hensley is a USA TODAY bestselling author of hot, dark and dirty romance. She is also an Amazon Top 10 best-selling author. Being a multi-published author in the romance genre, Alta is known for her dark, gritty alpha heroes, sometimes sweet love stories, hot eroticism, and engaging tales of the constant struggle between dominance and submission.

She lives in a log cabin in the woods with her husband, two daughters, and an Australian Shepherd. When she isn't battling the bats, and watching the deer, she is writing about villains who always get their love story and happily ever after.

Facebook: https://www.facebook.com/
AltaHensleyAuthor/
Amazon: https://www.amazon.com/Alta-Hensley/e/
B004G5A6LI
Website: www.altahensley.com
Instagram: https://instagram.com/altahensley
Bookbub: https://www.bookbub.com/authors/alta-hensley
TikTok: https://www.tiktok.com/@altahensley
Join her mailing list: https://landing.mailerlite.com/
webforms/landing/c9b6n3

About Renee Rose

USA TODAY BESTSELLING AUTHOR RENEE ROSE loves a dominant, dirty-talking alpha hero! She's sold over two million copies of steamy romance with varying levels of kink. Her books have been featured in USA Today's *Happily Ever After* and *Popsugar*. Named Eroticon USA's Next Top Erotic Author in 2013, she has also won *Spunky and Sassy's* Favorite Sci-Fi and Anthology author, *The Romance Reviews* Best Historical Romance, and *has* hit the *USA Today* list over a dozen times with her Chicago Bratva, Bad Boy Alpha and Wolf Ranch series, as well as various anthologies.

Renee loves to connect with readers!
www.reneeroseromance.com
renee@reneeroseromance.com

facebook.com/reneeroseromance

twitter.com/reneeroseauthor

instagram.com/reneeroseromance

amazon.com/Renee-Rose/e/B008AS0FT0

bookbub.com/authors/renee-rose

tiktok.com/@authorreneerose